COO 406 366X

Teenager

Gangs
Bullying

DUNDEE CITY COUNCIL

CENTRAL LIBRARY

SCHOOL LIBRARY SERVICE

Dundee

Education

D1465016

By the same author
Love, Shelley

K. Saksena

BLOOMSBURY

DUNDEE CITY
COUNCIL

LOCATION

Schools

ACCESSION NUMBER

COO 406 366X

SUPPLIER | PRICE

Bert | £5.99

CLASS No. | DATE
016 | 20/10/05

First published in Great Britain in 2005 by Bloomsbury Publishing Plc
38 Soho Square, London, W1D 3HB

Copyright © 2005 Kate Saksena
The moral right of the author has been asserted

All rights reserved
No part of this publication may be reproduced or
transmitted by any means, electronic, mechanical, photocopying
or otherwise, without the prior permission of the publisher

A CIP catalogue record of this book is available from the British Library

ISBN 0 7475 6899 5

All papers used by Bloomsbury Publishing are natural, recyclable products made from wood
grown in well-managed forests. The manufacturing processes conform to the environmental
regulations of the country of origin.

Typeset by Dorchester Typesetting Group Ltd
Printed in Great Britain by Clays Ltd, St Ives plc

1 3 5 7 9 10 8 6 4 2

www.bloomsbury.com/hite

For my son

Chapter 1

Dad

'Leave him, Ted,' said his mum.

'Keep out of it, you,' hissed his dad.

'But the boy's –'

'I said shut it.' His voice was louder. Lee could see the spit spray as he spoke. His mum turned to him, her eyes sad and hopeless, and then she went out of the room and shut the door.

'Now, you.'

Dad turned. Lee took a step back but Dad grabbed him and held him still. His hands felt like a vice, he was gripping so hard.

'This is the second time they've phoned this week. I told them I'd sort it out on Monday. Now you've done it again. What have you got to say?'

Lee said nothing. He stared down at the floor. If I keep still enough, he was thinking, he'll loosen his grip and I can get away.

'Well? Answer me!' said his dad.

Lee continued his silence.

'You stubborn little git,' he shouted. 'Say something!'

He started shaking Lee by the shoulders. Then he stopped abruptly.

'Look, son.' He tried to make his voice gentler, more reasonable. Lee could sense the strain this involved. 'You've got to go to school. Your teachers said you've got learning difficulties. That means you need more school, not less.'

'I don't learn much at school,' said Lee sulkily.

'I don't care what you learn at school, you've got to go. You're thirteen. You can't leave till you're sixteen, and I'm not paying fines or having busybodies knocking at the door chasing you. Is that clear?'

Lee was silent.

'Right, I'll have to march you down to the school gate every morning, then.'

'No … no …' said Lee, horrified at the thought of arriving at school with his dad.

'Ashamed of me then, are you?'

He stared miserably at the floor.

'I shouldn't expect you to go to school like normal children, should I? It's my own fault for marrying the daughter of a bloody pikey. No learning. No respect.

It's your mother's influence. Or your mad witch of a grandmother.'

He paused. He was breathing heavily. His eyes flashed angrily. He pulled Lee right up to him so that his feet only just touched the ground and his face was close, too close. Close enough to see the red veins in his eyes, the blotchy skin, the little tufts of hair protruding from his nose and ears. Close enough to smell the staleness of his breath, the pub odour of his clothes.

'I'm telling you, Lee. If you hop school again I won't be able to keep my temper, like I'm doing now. Do you understand?'

Lee nodded vigorously. Anything to get out of this horrible closeness. His dad's grip weakened and he was standing firmly on the floor once more. He waited. He expected a slap or a punch or 'a belt round the ear' as his dad called it. But Dad just turned away with a loud sigh and flopped on to his chair in front of the telly.

'Go on,' he snarled. 'Get out of my sight before I belt you.'

Lee needed no persuasion. He rushed for the door and ran down the hall and out of the front door. He didn't want to wait for the lift. Waiting seemed too risky. He needed to run. Up he went, one, two, three, four, five, six flights of stairs, then through the emergency door whose lock he had managed to break the previous month. Up the narrow, dark steps inside and through another smaller door. He closed it behind him and leaned against it, breathing heavily. Then he took a gulp of air and climbed across to the little area he had made his own. He flopped down, gazed around and smiled.

Rockwell House was a five-storey block of flats. It was an ugly building of dirt-streaked concrete and peeling paintwork. Around it were other similar blocks, separated by car parks and tiny triangles of grass. It was a depressing, grey sort of place. But up here it was bearable. Up here, on the roof, all the little nastinesses of life seemed far away. Just as the cars and the people seemed smaller, so did the arguments and the problems. When he'd first found his way on to the roof, he'd been surprised by all the rubbish that various workmen had left up there – cables, bits of wood and two old doors. Last week it had been cold and wet, so he'd dragged the doors over to the chimneystack, which was always warm, and leaned them together to make a little shelter. The previous day he'd brought up an old blanket, and now the little space looked cosy and inviting and safe. But first he stood gazing about him.

Immediately around was the Morden estate he knew so well. Beyond, was the main road and the shops. He could see the park, the allotments where his granddad used to dig and plant, and, further away, the tall building where the council offices were. In the distance were the high office blocks of Croydon, and in the other direction was the hill on which the Crystal Palace masts sat like watchtowers, guarding the sprawl of south London at their feet. Lee stretched out his arms and lifted his face to the sky. This was what he liked most, to feel the wind on his face, in his hair, cooling the helpless rage his dad made him feel.

He went to the other side of the chimneystack and moved a heavy wedge of broken concrete. Underneath, wrapped in an old carrier bag, was a little sketchbook. A drizzly rain was beginning to fall, veiling Croydon's skyline and the guardian masts. Lee crawled into the space under the old door, tucked the blanket around him and, taking a stubby pencil from his pocket, he began to draw.

It was only when he could hardly see his pencil that he realised darkness had fallen. He left his little hut and strolled across the roof, gazing at the lines of streetlights below. He could never quite decide which he liked best: the daytime, when he could see for miles and when he could clearly identify below him the world he inhabited, or night, when the lights twinkled, lending an air of excitement and glamour, and he could gaze at the moon and the tiny patterns of stars.

There were no stars yet, it was too early. It was beginning to get cold and the earlier drizzle was turning to rain. He crept through the door and, taking care not to be seen, he quickly ran downstairs. He didn't stop on the first floor except to check there was no one in sight. He didn't want to go home. Not yet.

Outside, he wandered through the wet streets watching the people rushing home, heads drawn like tortoises' inside hoods or under umbrellas. He watched the traffic, shining with rain, drivers peering from behind their windscreen wipers. He noticed how the lights were reflected, wobbly and fragmented, in the puddles and wet shop windows. He turned into a narrower, darker street and knocked on the door of a small house. The door opened very quickly.

'I thought you would be here,' said a low, lilting voice.

'Hi, Della,' said Lee.

'You're drenched,' the old lady said. 'Where's your coat?'

'I ... I forgot it,' said Lee.

'Or rushed out in a state and didn't have time to get it.'

Lee grinned sheepishly at his grandmother. She moved closer to him, frowning.

'There's a shadow on your shoulder, Lee. Have you had another row with your father?'

'Sort of,' sighed Lee.

'Come. You need to get into the warm and take that wet sweater off. Go and find an old jumper of your granddad's to wear while it's drying. I'll make some tea.'

Lee went upstairs. On the first-floor landing were two doors. He went into the larger of the two bed-rooms and opened a drawer. Inside, Granddad's clothes lay clean and neatly folded. They seemed to be waiting for him to wear them. But Granddad had been dead for two years. Lee always felt a little strange in this room since Granddad's death. It felt as if he was trespassing. Della had told him that was nonsense. But he felt it again now. An uneasiness. Perhaps it was just sadness that his granddad wasn't around any more. He took out a green jumper and pulled it on, welcoming the warmth.

Downstairs in the cluttered living room, Della had already placed a little tray on one of the many small tables. There were cups of tea and a plate of cakes and biscuits. Lee sat down. A warm rush of comfort and well-being enveloped him.

'What was it about this time?' Della asked.

'School,' said Lee, biting into a chocolate cake.

'Have you skipped school again?' she asked.

'Yeah.'

'Why?'

'You know why. I hate it.'

'Where did you go?'

'Nowhere,' replied Lee evasively.

Della didn't probe any further. She sat back, sipping her tea and watching him closely. She was a tiny, bird-like woman. Her face was lined and had that papery skin of the elderly but her hair was raven-black, as were her clothes. Lee sat, relaxed, eating cake and sipping tea. Often, with Della, they would sit in comfortable silence, not feeling the need to speak. Lee thought, secretly, that this was because Della could read his thoughts, so there was no need for her to talk to him.

She leaned forwards and picked up a little box from the table in front of her. It was a carved wooden box, one that Lee knew well. From it she took a pack of cards, wrapped in a piece of black silk. They were old and dog-eared. She held them in her hand and then, staring at Lee, she began to shuffle them slowly and methodically. After a few moments she handed them to Lee. He shuffled them in the same methodical way, then divided them into seven piles, put them back into a pack again and handed them to her.

Della placed the little pack in front of her, then laid the cards out in a cross shape.

'There it is again,' she sighed.

In the middle of the cross was an ornate picture of two young knights sitting playing chess outside a tent. In front of them were four swords lying on the ground. Lee knew it was a disturbing card. In fact he knew everything about that card.

'Lee,' said Della gently. 'We must find a way out of this.'

Chapter 2

Darren

Lee was woken by his mum shaking him.

'Come on, Lee. I've made some breakfast. You've got to get to school today.'

Lee opened his eyes just enough to look around. His mum, bulky in her fluffy pink dressing-gown, was shaking his brother Darren awake.

'Come on, both of you, into the kitchen.'

Darren struggled out of bed and threw on his school uniform. Lee couldn't yet bring himself to leave the warmth. Darren turned when he got to the door.

'Please get up, Lee. You know what Dad's like if you stay in bed.'

Darren was a scrawny, nervous boy of eight. He looked even more nervous that morning. Lee felt guilty. He slid out of the bed and padded along to the kitchen, where his mother was huddled over a teapot. She pushed some toast towards him.

'You will stay at school today, won't you?'

Lee, his mouth full of toast, said nothing.

'Promise me you'll go to school and stay there today!'

He tried but failed to avoid her eyes.

'OK, Mum,' he promised reluctantly.

Half an hour later, he was on his way to school. As he approached, the urge to bolt became stronger and stronger. Everywhere there were groups of boys and girls, laughing, shouting, arguing, whispering. He couldn't see anyone else walking by themselves. I must go in, he was thinking. If I don't, it won't just be me that gets it in the neck. He gritted his teeth and went through the side door.

'Hello, stranger,' said a sarcastic voice. It was one of the girls in his class. He turned and walked in the other direction, away from the form room. His nerve was giving way. He had that dizzy feeling. He needed to get out. He started running. But on the stairs someone stopped him. A hand rested on his shoulder.

'Good morning, Lee.'

He expected to be told off for running, told off for bunking school.

'It's nice to see you,' continued the voice. Lee looked up and saw Jean, his support teacher. 'Come and tell Miss Barratt you're here today. She'll be very pleased.'

He was gently, but firmly, ushered to a room on the first floor, a comfortable, friendly room. It had easy chairs in one corner and computers in another. The walls were always bright and there was often music playing. It was the only room in the school that he liked.

'Come and sit down over here,' said Jean, and she led him to the comfy chairs.

Jean brought Lee here, to the Progress Room, several times a week and helped him with his reading and writing. He liked those sessions, especially when Jean was helping him and no one else. He sat down. Miss Barratt, who was in charge of the room, came out of her tiny office and smiled at him.

'Nice to see you. We've missed you, Lee.'

She said it in a nice way but he didn't really believe she meant it. How could she? What did she care?

'I've got a question to ask you,' she said.

Lee stared at her, suspicious.

'Jean and I realise that you've found school difficult recently. Do you agree?'

Lee nodded, warily.

'We want you in school, Lee, so I'm suggesting

that, for today only, you spend the whole day with us here.'

He looked at her. What was the catch?

'Would you stay in school if you were in this room with Jean all day?'

Lee nodded.

'Then that's settled. But remember, it's only for today. Tomorrow we need to get you back to some of your lessons.'

Lee was surprised. He'd expected to get into trouble. Not with Jean, she was always nice to him, but he'd expected trouble from the other teachers.

Soon, however, he was busy and forgot to worry. Time went quickly. At the end of the day he was allowed to play some computer games because he'd worked so hard, and he went home almost cheerful.

He found Mum sitting watching television, her knitting on her lap. Dad was at work.

'You did stay at school today, didn't you?' asked Mum.

'Of course. I promised, didn't I?'

'Good lad.'

'Where's Darren?'

'He's gone to buy some milk.'

Lee was surprised. Darren didn't like going out on

his own. He usually stayed in and watched TV or played in their room. He thought he'd go and find him. He changed quickly, grabbed a packet of crisps and went out. He walked along to the shop. There was no sign of Darren. He went in – still no sign. The shopkeeper looked at him suspiciously, so he left. Where was Darren? Lee knew all the places where the local kids gathered. He usually tried to avoid them. He ran round the back of Rockwell House. There he saw a group of older boys smoking and smashing beer bottles against the wall. He ran off quickly, before they saw him. Down at the far end of the car park, behind an old caravan, he saw another group. He crept up behind the caravan. He couldn't see them, but he could hear them. Darren was there.

'Why don't you come out with us more often, then, baby boy?' a jeering girl's voice was demanding.

'Probably thinks he's much better than us,' said another.

'Are we too common for you then, Darren Highsmith?' the first girl went on.

'Well we can't be too clever for him. Look at how thick his brother is!' They all laughed.

How many were there? Lee peeped round the corner. Four, two boys, two girls. They were younger than him, but bigger. He stood quivering, listening.

'What about you, Darren? You look like you take after your brother. You're a scrawny little rat like him. Are you as thick as him as well?'

Darren said nothing.

'And as weird! Lee's a bloody psycho. He's always running out of school.'

'Yeah. You'd be better off sticking with us, Darren. Your brother's a loser.'

'Oh, God, what a wimp. He's crying!'

'That's pathetic. We only wanted to have a little chat.'

'But wasn't he on his way to the shop?'

'Oh yeah. Darren, you wouldn't have a couple of quid to lend your friends, would you?'

Darren must have shaken his head.

'Come on, don't be so mean. You won't have any friends if you don't share things with them.'

Lee thought he heard a struggle.

'Oh, look,' said a triumphant voice. 'Our friend's found a pound for his mates. Well done, Darren. That's really sweet of you. Now beat it.'

Lee slipped away from the caravan and crouched behind a car. He saw Darren dart across the car park. He waited a moment, then ran after him. He caught him up at the door of the flats. Darren's little face was red and tear-stained. He was biting his lip.

'What's Mum going to say?' sobbed Darren. 'I haven't got any milk.'

'With a bit of luck, she won't remember you going to get any. Just go into the bedroom and look like you've been there all along. Come on, don't worry. Dad isn't there.'

'Not now, but he'll be home later, and if there's no milk, it'll all be my fault.'

Lee dragged Darren reluctantly up to the flat and they crept in quietly. Lee remembered Della giving him some money the day before.

'Stay here,' he whispered. 'I'll go and get some milk.'

'But that lot'll get you as well!'

'No they won't. I know where they are. I'll sneak out the back way. They won't see me.'

'Be careful,' said Darren and threw himself miserably on to his bunk.

When Lee got home, he put the milk in the fridge and Darren went to join his mum in the living room. Lee stood at the door, watching. Mum smiled at Darren and carried on knitting. Relieved, Lee went out, racing up the steps to his rooftop sanctuary.

Snuggled into his little shelter, gazing out over the suburban sprawl, he wished his life was different. Why did he have to live with Dad, when he knew that Della had offered to take him in lots of times? Why was school so horrible? Why couldn't he be one of those people who liked school? And why was he so small for his age? Some of the boys in his class were like big men, with hairy arms and shadow on their lips. They were tall and muscular. He seemed to be the same size as when he'd started that school. If he was big and tall he wouldn't get all that flak from the others in his class, he'd be able to fight back. He'd be able to take Dad on when he started on him. Best of all, he'd be able to stop the other kids making Darren's life a misery.

He kicked angrily at the chimneystack. It was beginning to get dark. Lights were going on in the world below. Strips of streetlights and the red and white lines of cars. The sight made Lee feel a little calmer. He got out his sketchbook and the stubby bit of pencil. He was just about to start drawing when a familiar sound made him start. The door on to the roof was being pushed open.

Chapter 3

Chicken Slices

Lee was crouching behind the chimneystack when the figure came into view. He expected a workman or a caretaker or someone who'd seen him come up to the roof and wanted to have a go at him. But the figure was a girl. She was older than him, probably eighteen or twenty. She had a woolly hat covering her hair, a big army jacket and boots. On her back she was carrying a rucksack.

Lee had never seen her before. He watched suspiciously. She paced about, looking carefully around. She examined the satellite dishes and aerials, looked at the water tank and stared at the view from all sides. Then she came towards Lee and he knew she was examining his little hiding place. He heard paper being turned. She must be looking at his sketchbook. He didn't want anyone looking at his sketchbook!

Then, straining his ears, he realised that she was

settling herself into his little hiding place and opening her rucksack. He had a sinking feeling. She'd obviously come to stay. She was taking over his private domain.

Lee sat quietly fuming, trying to decide what to do. If he spoke to her, told her it was his place, she'd probably just laugh at him. She might be angry. She might be completely mad and push him over the edge of the roof. But, if he didn't do anything, she might take over completely. Then where would he go? He decided, on balance, it would be safer to say nothing until he knew a bit more about her. He sat a while longer listening, but she made no sound. He looked about miserably. The roof wasn't the same with someone else there. He slipped over to the door and went home.

As soon as he went in he regretted it. Dad was home. He could hear him shouting in the kitchen. It sounded as if he'd been drinking. Lee tiptoed into his bedroom and found Darren lying on his bunk playing with a Gameboy.

'Are you all right?' asked Lee.

'Yeah. I just came in here when I heard him come home. He's drunk again.'

'He's always drunk these days. But it's a bit early. Why hasn't he stayed till closing time?'

'I think that's what he's shouting about. He's run out of money.'

It was Thursday. Dad got paid on Saturdays. That meant life would be unbearable for the next two days. Lee climbed up to his bunk and lay wishing he was on the roof. There he could lie and gaze at the sky and the stars. Here all he could see was the bumpy textured paint and the huge crack across the ceiling. If he stretched out his hand he could burn his fingers on the old blue lampshade.

'Have you had any tea?' he asked.

'No. Mum said she'd make some cheese on toast, but then he came in.'

Lee could hear his stomach rumbling. He tried to think of something else to take his mind off food. He thought about the girl on the roof. What was she doing there? Was she homeless and planning to live there? Was she a drug addict wanting somewhere quiet to take her drugs? Was she running away from something and hiding there? Was she a criminal, on the run from the police – a murderer perhaps, or someone escaped from a psychiatric hospital? Someone like Hannibal Lecter in that film.

There was one way of finding out, but not until tomorrow. The voices in the kitchen suddenly became louder. They must have opened the door.

'Lee,' called his father's voice, thick with alcohol. 'Come here!'

Lee wondered what he'd done wrong now. For a second, he considered hiding, but decided against it.

'Lee,' his father shouted impatiently.

He slid down off his bed and went to the door of the kitchen. His mum was sitting at the table. She looked tired and anxious.

'Come and help us,' said his dad. 'The writing on this is too small for me to read and your mum says she's lost her glasses. Can you read this?'

He handed Lee a long thin piece of paper. It was a till receipt from the supermarket. Lee glanced at the total figure at the bottom – £73.

'What do you want me to read?'

'All of it,' said Dad.

Lee glanced at it nervously. He could see lots of words he wasn't familiar with. The back of his neck started to prickle and his palms were suddenly damp.

'Eggs – half a dozen,' he began, reading slowly and carefully. 'Large white loaf – three, 250g tomato sauce, chicken slices –'

'Chicken slices,' repeated Dad. 'And where are they, then?'

'The boys had them for tea the other day,' said Mum, almost in a whisper.

'Oh, I see,' said Dad. 'The boys get chicken slices! And what do I get? No matter. I'm just the one who brings home the money. Didn't think to save me some chicken slices, did you? Probably ate them all yourself. Look at you. You're getting fat! You probably stuff yourself with food all day when I'm working. Go on, Lee, let's see what the fat cow's been buying to stuff her face with.'

Lee looked from his mother's blank, miserable face to his father's flushed and angry one. He didn't want to be here. He wanted the ground to open up. He wanted to be up on his roof and out of this.

'Go on!' yelled Dad.

'500g sugar, baked beans – 2 tins, baked beans with pork sausages – 2 tins –'

'Hold on, hold on. There's another thing. Where have these baked beans with sausages got to? Yesterday you gave me baked beans, ordinary baked beans, no sign of a sausage. Who gets the beans with the sausages in?'

His mother said nothing.

'Lee, do you eat those?' he demanded.

'Not usually,' said Lee. 'We usually have just beans.' It was a lie. They'd had beans and sausages the day before, but he didn't want to get his mum into trouble. His plan backfired.

'So you're not giving them to me and you're not giving them to the boys. I suppose you're scoffing them, too, you greedy cow. What will it be next? You'll be buying yourself cream cakes and chocolates and bloody bouquets of flowers! Go on, Lee.'

Lee glanced at his mum but there was no response. She was staring into space.

'Fruit salad, tinned, m … m … g …'

'What?'

Lee was stumbling. He couldn't work it out.

'M … g …'

'Read it, you idiot!' screamed his dad.

Lee knew he wouldn't be able to now. He was hot and flustered and his eyes, his mouth and his brain had stopped working together.

'I can't believe this,' said Dad. 'Not only have I got a fat, lazy wife who eats away all my hard-earned cash but I've also got a son who's an idiot. Can't even read! How long have you been going to school, Lee? I'll tell you – nine years – and you can't even read the shopping bill!'

'Leave him, Ted,' said Mum.

Dad looked like he'd been punched. He pulled himself up so that he looked taller and put his hands on his hips.

'Don't you tell me what to do or say to my own kids. Just shut it, woman. Read the list, Lee.'

Lee was silent. His head was spinning.

'I said read it!' his dad hissed, stepping nearer to him.

Lee stared blindly at the shopping list.

'This is stupid,' he said quietly, and put the list on the table.

'Pick the thing up and read it!' shouted his dad furiously, lurching a step nearer.

Lee, remembering Darren's desperate face earlier that day, did nothing.

'I said pick it up.'

Dad was close to him again. Lee, his heart racing, his skin prickling, stared at his dad. He didn't move.

'You illiterate, stupid moron,' spat his dad. 'I'll teach you to do as I say!'

He grabbed Lee's sweatshirt with one hand, with the other he hit Lee in the face. Mum gasped. Lee turned to run but Dad still had hold of his top. He swung another punch at him, this time hitting him a glancing blow across the side of his forehead. The force of the blow made Dad stumble against the kitchen table. He loosened his grip to break his fall and Lee got away. He ran out of the kitchen and out of the flat.

On the landing he began to run up to the roof, then stopped abruptly. He couldn't. That girl would be there. He ran downstairs instead. It was dark and raining hard. Outside he kept running, his eyes blinded by rain and tears, his nose bleeding, his ears stinging, his head throbbing from the force of the blows. He didn't stop until he got to the dark little street.

His grandmother opened the door almost as soon as he got there. She said nothing. She led him to the fire, pulled his top off and wrapped an old dressing-gown round him. A few minutes later she brought 'cotton wool for your nose, hot chocolate for your spirits and a little drop of whisky to revive your poor bruised soul'.

Lee smiled, wincing at the pain in his cheek, and snuggled into the chair. Della stroked his head for a moment and pointed to the table. On it was a cross of cards. In the middle was a dark and menacing-looking card, with three arms in a circular pattern, each holding a vicious-looking sword. He felt a moment of alarm and looked at Della quizzically. She smiled. He gazed again at the card and saw how pleasing and neat the pattern was. For some reason it cheered him up.

Chapter 4

Vivienne

Lee woke early the next morning when Della came in with a cup of tea.

'Your mother's here,' she said.

'Mum? Why?'

'She's brought your school uniform and she wants to see how you are.'

Lee touched his nose and winced.

'What does it look like?'

'Like someone hit you,' said Della.

Lee jumped out of bed and went to the mirror. His lip was slightly swollen and there were bruises on his forehead and cheek.

'I can't go to school like this,' he said.

'But you can have some breakfast. Come on. Your mum's cooking you some eggs.'

In the kitchen his mum stared tearfully at his bruised face.

'I've fried some eggs for you,' she said and busied

herself serving them.

'Are you all right?' asked Lee.

'I'm fine.'

'And Darren?'

'Darren's fine too. He's on his way to school.'

'I can't go to school, Mum.'

'You must, Lee.'

'What am I going to say?'

'Say you had a fight with some kids.'

'They'll want details. Everyone wants details if there's been a fight.'

'Try and think of something, Lee.'

He ate his eggs in silence.

'You will go, won't you?'

'I'll go, but I'm still not sure what to say.'

'You'll think of something,' said Mum. 'You always had a good imagination.'

Lee walked to school quickly. He thought if he walked slowly, he'd be too tempted to take a different route. He tried to concentrate on what to say to explain his bruises. The idea of a fight was too complicated. He decided on an accident, a fall. He'd have to have fallen on something. What could he think of that sounded believable? He remembered other times when he'd been to school with bruises and said he'd fallen downstairs or walked into cupboards. He'd better not use those again.

He was at the school gates. Should he go to the classroom or to the Progress Room where he'd spent the day yesterday?

'What happened, Lee? Did you walk into a bus?' said a boy nearby. His friends laughed.

'No,' said Lee, surprising himself. 'I fell off a roof.'

The boy looked as if he was going to say something else but Lee walked off before he could. What have I said? A roof? Why did I say that? Now I'll have to stick with it.

He went into the Progress Room. Jean was there.

'Lee, what happened to you?' she said in concern.

'I fell off a roof,' repeated Lee.

'A roof? It's a wonder you didn't kill yourself! How did it happen?'

This was the question he was dreading. What had Mum said to him? He had a good imagination. Suddenly a picture came into his mind.

'It wasn't a high roof. It was only a shed. My grandmother's shed's all covered in ivy and it's getting ruined so she asked me to help her clear the ivy off. Then I fell and hit my head on one of those big flowerpots.'

'Ouch,' said Jean. 'Did you get it seen by a doctor?'

'No, my grandmother's good at that sort of thing.'

'Well, remember, if you get headaches, you need to see a doctor.'

'Don't worry, I'm fine. I just look a mess. Can I stay here today?'

'Not all day, Lee. There are too many others here on Fridays. You can stay for lesson one but then you must go to maths. That'll be all right. You like maths.'

'But after that it's English and geography.'

'You're going to have to go to them.'

'But I hate them!'

'Sorry, Lee.'

During maths, Lee was plagued with questions about his bruises. He was quite pleased with his story, so he stuck to it. One of the girls did say, 'Are you sure your old man didn't take a swing at you?' but Lee just shrugged and shook his head.

Things took a turn for the worse during English. His teacher was called Mr Vaughn and he had a loud voice and a fat belly. Lee hated him. When Mr Vaughn called the register at the beginning of the lesson, he stopped at Lee's name.

'Mr Highsmith,' he said sarcastically. 'You're actually present today. That's remarkable. You've made me do the register wrong. I've got so used to you being absent, I marked it in automatically.'

Lee said nothing.

'I counted twenty-three examples in all your books of you using "their", "there" and "they're" incorrectly,' Mr Vaughn said. 'So today we're going to practise and we'll keep practising until you all get it right. Billy, write them all on the board.'

Billy wrote the three words and Mr Vaughn labelled them a – there, b – their, c – they're. He reminded them which was which. Then, to Lee's dismay, he started to go round the class, giving each person a phrase like 'there is a park down the road', and they had to decide whether the sentence used a, b or c.

Lee was in the middle of the classroom. By the time Mr Vaughn reached Vivienne, the girl next to him, three people had got the wrong answer. Mr Vaughn had given them another until they got it right. Lee had a vision of Mr Vaughn giving him sentences all lesson, all day, all week because he couldn't ever get it right.

'Lee,' he bellowed. '"The girls said they're in the

library."' Lee hesitated. He felt that familiar sensation of prickling skin and clammy hands. His brain stopped working. His mouth opened, then closed. He had no idea. He couldn't even remember the phrase now. It was to do with girls in the library.

'Come on, Lee,' said Mr Vaughn.

'B,' said Lee wildly.

'Oh dear, Lee.' Mr Vaughn shook his head. 'That's not right. Now if you were here more often, you'd probably have learnt it by now. Let's try again.'

Again Lee imagined days of this torture stretching ahead.

'"They all like their Christmas presents."'

Lee repeated the sentence in his head. It was no good. He could never think properly when people put him on the spot like this. He looked desperately at the desk.

There was nothing there to help him but he noticed that Vivienne was holding her pen in a very peculiar way. Then he saw it. She was making a 'b' shape with her pen and her fingers.

'B,' he said.

'Well done, Lee. You see how quickly you catch on when you're actually in school?'

He passed on to the next person and Lee breathed

a sigh of relief. He picked up his pen and scrawled 'thanks' on the back of his rough book.

Geography was worse. Miss Green yelled, 'What on earth happened to you, Lee?' as soon as he walked in.

'He fell off a roof, Miss,' explained a nosy, loud girl called Michelle.

'Sounds very careless,' said Miss Green.

The class was working on something complicated about rainfall and Lee couldn't really follow it. He spent most of the lesson gazing out of the window. The geography room was on the third floor and from it he could see his block of flats. He stared at the roof, wondering if the strange girl was still squatting in his shelter.

'Have you done anything at all this lesson, Lee?' demanded Miss Green, who had suddenly appeared beside him.

'I was thinking, Miss,' said Lee.

'What exactly were you thinking of?'

'Rainfall,' said Lee, unexpectedly quick off the mark.

'Rainfall?'

'Yes. Look, it's raining outside.'

'Stop wasting time, Lee,' said Miss Green. 'What's the answer to this question?' She pointed to a page in his textbook.

Lee had no idea. He didn't really understand the question.

'I'm not sure,' he said.

'Then hurry up and work it out. You're not leaving the room till you've finished all of this section.'

Lee groaned. Unfortunately he wasn't sitting next to Vivienne, but a boy called Asaf who had only started school the week before and couldn't speak any English.

Lee read and re-read the page. Eventually he copied out some sentences as neatly as he could and hoped Miss Green wouldn't look too carefully. He was wrong. At the end of the lesson she stopped Lee and two others from leaving.

'Show me your work,' she ordered.

The first was told to sit and finish off, the second was told to leave, and then Lee showed her his book.

'What's this, Lee?' she demanded.

'My work, Miss,' he said.

'These aren't the answers to the questions.'

'But it is about rainfall.'

'It's copied, Lee.'

He was silent.

'You're never going to improve your work until

you try harder!' she said. 'Now sit down and answer the questions.'

Lee sat down. Again he had visions of time stretching endlessly ahead and him spending it all in the geography room. He was at a loss. What could he do?

Suddenly, there was a shout followed by wailing in the corridor and Miss Green rushed to the door. 'Don't you two move!' she warned as she left.

Lee didn't try to leave but he did take another pupil's book from the pile on the desk and copied the answers down quickly. The other boy followed his example and by the time she came back in they had finished.

Miss Green looked at them suspiciously but had to let them go.

At the end of school, Lee rushed home. He was so relieved to be out of school he forgot about what had happened the day before until he reached the door of the flat. His father's angry face flashed through his mind. Lee turned quickly away and ran up the steps, two at a time. At the top he pushed open the door to the roof with a huge sense of freedom and relief.

'Hello,' said a voice he'd never heard before.

Chapter 5

Ruby

Lee froze. He stared in horror at the figure standing facing him.

'What's the matter? Haven't you ever seen a girl on a roof before?'

Lee was speechless. He couldn't believe that he'd been so stupid, bursting through the door when he knew she might be up here.

She sat down, leaning against the wall. 'My name's Ruby, what's yours?'

Lee frowned and moved away slightly.

'What do you think I'm going to do? Bite?'

He sat down some distance from her and stared. She had the same big army boots, but today she wasn't wearing a woolly hat. She had long red hair, not a natural sort of ginger, but bright scarlet. It wasn't only the hair that made her look unusual. She had rows of rings in her ears, her nose and some in her eyebrows and she seemed to be staring at him as intensely as he was staring at her. Their eyes met. She smiled. It was a nice, warm smile, with lots of teeth showing.

'Now that you've seen what I look like, will you speak to me? I told you my name's Ruby. What's yours?'

Lee wasn't quite ready to answer. Then she smiled again.

'Lee,' he said.

'And what are you doing up here, Lee?'

'It's my roof,' he said, defensively.

'I see,' she replied thoughtfully. 'Is that your little shelter?'

He nodded.

'You saw me in there yesterday, didn't you?'

He nodded again.

'Were you cross?'

'I suppose.'

'Why didn't you say something?'

'I didn't know who you were.'

'You still don't.'

'But yesterday, I thought you might be dangerous.'

'And today?'

'You don't seem very dangerous.'

'Appearances can be deceptive, Lee.'

Lee shrugged. 'Why are you here?' he asked. 'You don't live in these flats, do you?'

'No, I live over there.' She pointed to a neighbouring road. 'But I've had my eye on this roof for a while.'

'What do you want it for?'

'What do *you* want it for?' she repeated.

'I don't know. I like it here. It's quiet.'

'You draw up here, don't you? I looked at your sketchbook.'

'You shouldn't have.'

'I'm sorry. It was just lying there.'

'That's because you surprised me. I didn't have time to hide it.'

'You shouldn't be shy. Your cartoons are good. I wish I could draw.'

Lee was silent.

'You still haven't told me why you come up here,' he reminded her.

'Two reasons. One is the same as yours. I like to be away from other people, somewhere quiet.'

'What's the other reason?'

'It's the closest you can get to the sky around here.'

Lee looked up. She was right. It was one of the things that he liked about being so high up.

'Are you planning to live up here?' asked Lee.

'Of course not.' Ruby laughed. 'It would be freezing up here in the middle of winter.'

'Then when do you plan to come here?'

'When I have time. Don't worry, you probably won't even notice me.'

'Of course I will. You can't help noticing if someone else comes up here.'

'I don't mean that. I mean I probably won't be here when you are.'

Lee was puzzled.

'How do you know?'

'Because I'll probably only come up here at night,' she said.

Lee stared at her, confused.

'At night?' he repeated. 'Why?'

'Why not?'

'Well, no reason. But what are you going to do up here at night?'

'I'm going to lie down and look at the stars.' She got up and went to the other side of the building. 'Is this the highest roof you've been on?' she asked.

'Yeah, I think so,' answered Lee.

'Do you ever imagine being on a really tall building or a mountain top?'

'Sometimes.'

'And me,' she said dreamily. 'Anyway, I must go now.'

'Aren't you going to stay to see the stars?'

'No, I'm hungry. I'm going home to have my tea.' She started towards the door. 'Bye, Lee. Nice to have met you.'

'Bye,' he replied, but she was already gone.

He sat down in his little shelter, thinking about Ruby. What a strange girl. What did she want to come up here for? Surely girls of her age had other things to do? Why did she like to look at the sky? Then he smiled to himself. Why was he so puzzled? Was it so odd that someone else in the world liked it up on the roof?

Lee realised he was hungry, too. He went down to the flat and listened outside the door, wondering if his dad was there. He couldn't hear anything in particular, so he went in. Darren came into the hall to greet him.

'You're just in time, Lee. Mum's got some fish and chips.'

Lee was surprised. When he went into the kitchen Mum smiled and handed him a white parcel. He opened it and tucked in hungrily, deciding not to ask

Mum how she'd managed to afford it.

'Where's Dad?' he asked.

'Down the pub,' said Mum.

'But I thought –' he began.

'Don't ask questions, Lee. Just enjoy your tea.'

He did. He ate every piece of fish, every crunchy crumb of batter, every chip, including the little crispy bits that aren't quite chips. Mum had even bought a bottle of Coke to go with it.

Afterwards she put all the wrappers and the Coke bottle into a plastic bag and sent Lee out to dispose of it. When he came back, the kitchen window was open and the smell of fish was being swallowed up by the flowery scent of air freshener.

It was several hours later, when he and Darren were in bed, that he heard the sounds of a key not quite going into the keyhole, accompanied by a string of curses. At last the door creaked open and then slammed shut. A series of shuffles, crashes and curses marked Dad's movement along the corridor. There was a crash as he opened his bedroom door, then, mercifully, silence.

On Saturday morning Mum told Lee to look after his brother and take him out somewhere. She gave him five pounds to get some lunch. Darren wanted to go to a park. They wouldn't go to the park along the road. It was full of hard older kids. They decided to go to a different one. It had no playground but it did have paths you could skate on and a little river. Lee liked it.

They got to the bottom of the stairs at Rockwell House and saw a group of six boys. Lee recognised them instantly. The leader of the group was famous. His name was Yaz. They were all in their late teens, much older and much bigger than Lee and Darren. Lee paused on the stairs, hoping they could just stroll past the group, but Yaz had noticed them.

'Hi there, Lee,' he said smiling. 'How you doing, mate?'

'Fine,' said Lee, trying to sound relaxed. 'How you doing, Yaz?'

'I'm fit as a fiddle, Lee. Is that Darren you've got with you? Hi, Darren.'

Darren said, 'Hi', moving close to Lee's side.

'I'm really pleased we saw you two today,' Yaz continued, still smiling. 'It's a bit of luck, don't you think?' He turned to his mates, who nodded. 'You see, boys, we need a bit of help.'

Lee heard Darren take a sharp breath. Lee said nothing.

'You would like to help Yaz, wouldn't you?' said one of the other boys, taking a step closer towards them.

'Of course,' said Lee. 'But we're meant to be at my nan's house. Is it something we can help with later?'

'I'm afraid not,' the same boy said, smiling unpleasantly. 'I'm afraid Yaz needs your help right now.'

Lee saw it was impossible to avoid whatever it was Yaz had in mind. His mates were carefully positioned so that there was no way to get to the doors or the lifts. They were not the kind of boys you could argue with. Yaz himself was short and stocky with dyed blond hair and ropes of heavy gold chain on his chest. He was always dressed very smartly in black. Everyone knew he had a six-inch blade in his pocket. His right-hand man was a boy called Wilko. He was tall and wide with spiky ginger hair and a scorpion tattoo on his neck. His cheek bore the scar of a knife fight he'd been in the year before. The only other one Lee knew by name was a tall, thin, unsmiling black boy called Ty, who always wore a black woollen hat pulled down to his eyes.

'What do you want us to do, then?' Lee asked.

'I just need you to come and help me for a few

minutes. Come on, it's not far.'

Yaz turned and walked out. The others waited, watching Lee and Darren.

Lee said, 'I think Darren should go back. If we don't turn up at my nan's she'll phone and Mum will worry.'

'Yaz wants you both,' said Wilko, and Ty moved quietly behind Darren.

There was no escape. They went out and joined Yaz. He led them past the shops to a road beyond Della's. It was a narrow road of run-down houses. Some of them were boarded up.

Yaz put a hand on Lee's shoulder. He pointed to a house opposite.

'You see, Lee, that house belongs to my friend, but he's forgotten to return some things of mine that I need rather urgently.'

Lee looked. The curtains were closed and the house looked sad and neglected.

'Why can't you ask for them back?' asked Lee.

'Good question. Clever boy!' said Yaz, clapping him on the back. 'You see, he's gone away. He's … he's gone on holiday … abroad. And I need my things today.'

Lee was beginning to understand.

'What do you want me for?'

'Well, Wilko here has found a way in round the back, but you can see he's a big lad. He needs someone a bit slimmer to go in and open the door for us.'

Lee's heart was beating fast.

'Why don't you just break a window?'

'You see,' said Yaz, turning to his mates. 'I told you he was a bright boy. It's because my friend is a bit security-conscious. He's put bars on all the main windows. Now let's not hang about. Wilko, you take Lee round the back and show him.'

Lee looked at the terrified expression on Darren's face.

Yaz followed his gaze.

'Don't worry about Darren. I'll look after him. Now go with Wilko.'

Yaz's tone had changed. Wilko grabbed Lee's arm and led him up a narrow lane. He looked to check no one was around, then slid through a gate into a rubbish-filled yard.

They were at the back of the friend's house. Wilko pointed to a small window high up in what was probably the kitchen wall.

'You've got to climb through there,' he said.

Chapter 6

Wilko

Lee felt trapped. His instinct was to run. He was a fast runner. He could easily avoid Wilko, slide through the gate and get away.

'Don't even think it,' said Wilko, standing squarely in front of him, lighting up a cigarette. 'You see, Lee, if you don't manage this little job for us, we've got someone else who will.'

Lee stared at him, uncomprehending. Then the penny dropped. Of course, he meant Darren. So running away was not an option. He turned and gazed at the window.

'How can I reach it?' he asked.

'That's what I'm here for. You can stand on my shoulders.'

'But what about the glass?'

'We're going to break it.'

'But ...' Lee had visions of being slashed to pieces by broken glass as he squeezed through the window.

'Don't worry, Lee. You're not with a bunch of amateurs. Look, you just stand there and watch. I'll prepare the way.'

Lee watched with terrified fascination as Wilko dragged an old cupboard across the yard and climbed on to it. From there he could reach the window. From his coat pocket he got out a hammer and smashed the glass. Then he carefully knocked out all the little jagged pieces round the edge. But Lee could still see bits of glass sticking out. He was about to say something when Wilko delved into his jacket again and brought out a reel of thick tape. He carefully stuck the tape all round the edges of the window, covering the remaining shards of glass. In some places he stuck several layers. Then he got down and pushed the cupboard to the side.

'Come on. I've done the tricky stuff. Now you do the easy bit.'

'What do I do?'

'Get on my shoulders and slither through the window on to the cupboard inside. Then jump down and go into the hall. There's a cupboard behind the door. Open it and take out the bunch of keys. All you've got to do is pass them to Yaz through the letterbox.'

Lee stared at the window and then at Wilko.

There was something bothering him. What was it?

'Gloves!' he said suddenly. 'You've got gloves on. If I don't wear gloves I'll leave fingerprints. I'll get caught!'

'Have the police got your prints?' asked Wilko.

'No.'

'Then how are they going to identify you?'

Lee could see the logic of this but it didn't stop him worrying.

Wilko watched him for a minute.

'OK. If it makes you happy, wear the gloves and give them back to me at the front door.'

Lee put on the enormous gloves and climbed on to the cupboard in front of him. Wilko crouched down, his back towards Lee, his arms held up.

'Hold my hands,' he said. 'Now climb on to my shoulders and steady yourself. Then I'll stand up.'

Lee climbed effortlessly on to his shoulders and Wilko, puffing like a weightlifter, stood up. Lee could see into the kitchen now. It was a very messy kitchen. He grabbed the side of the window carefully and pushed his head through. The cupboard was, as Wilko said, just below, and high enough for him to slide on to it without crashing down. He took a deep breath and dived. He'd done it. He was half lying on a battered old cupboard which didn't feel too secure. He twisted round and jumped on to the floor, crossed to the door and opened it. As he did so he froze.

There were sounds from the next room. Little sounds. It was paper rustling. The door was open. What should he do? If there was someone there, why hadn't they rushed into the kitchen when the glass smashed? This thought made him bolder. He eased himself forwards and peeped into the room. There was no one there. He must be imagining things. No, there it was again, a funny rustling sound. He went further into the room, following the noise. Suddenly he froze again as something moved. Once he'd caught his breath, he almost smiled. It was a rat. A smallish brown rat, now scurrying away.

Lee turned back to the hall with one aim – to get this over with as quickly as possible. He found the cupboard. It had several little drawers in, which were awkward to open in the big thick gloves. But at last he found a bunch of about six keys. He opened the letterbox in the front door and peered through. To his surprise the gang were not outside. His heart beat even faster. Where were they? Had he been set up? Then Yaz came into view, with Darren close behind him.

'Have you got them?' demanded Yaz, as he reached the door.

'Yeah. I thought you'd gone off and left me!' said Lee.

'There was someone walking past, so we went for a little walk, didn't we, Darren?' explained Yaz unpleasantly. 'Now pass those keys.'

Lee passed them through and Yaz deftly found the right ones and opened the door. They all trooped in.

'Well done, Lee,' said Wilko. 'You can go now.'

'Hang about,' said Yaz. 'I think you need to give our little mates some ... uh ... advice, don't you, Wilko.'

Wilko grinned. 'Remember, you two. You weren't here, you don't know us, you saw nothing. Is that clear?'

The two boys nodded.

'A bit clearer, Wilks,' said Yaz.

'What Yaz means, lads,' went on Wilko, 'is that if you ever squeaked a word of this to anyone, he'd smash your skulls to a pulp. Is that clear enough, Yaz?'

'I think that'll do. Now get lost, you two.'

Lee grabbed Darren's arm and started running down the street. Then he heard the sound of someone running after them. He turned in alarm to see the silent Ty bearing down on them. What was he going to do? Once again Lee's first instinct was to run, but this was not the rather overweight Wilko. Ty looked fit and fast. Lee stopped. Ty ran up to them.

'What now?' asked Lee.

Ty said nothing. He simply pointed at Lee's hands. Lee realised he still had Wilko's huge gloves on. He handed them over, relieved that Ty was only after the gloves.

When he'd gone they both turned and ran. They ran fast and in silence until Darren finally put out his hand and they paused, breathless, clutching their sides, on a bridge over a shallow stream.

'Where are we going, Lee?' puffed Darren.

Lee looked at his brother, his eyes big with fear, his face red with the effort of running.

'You wanted a day in the park, didn't you?' Lee said, between gasps.

They set off again, at a gentler pace. When they reached the park, Lee bought two bumper hot dogs, covered with onions and tomato sauce. They sat on a bench and ate as if they hadn't been fed for weeks. It was only when they'd finished that they spoke about what had happened.

'What did you have to do?' asked Darren.

Lee told him, very briefly.

'Could you get arrested for doing that?' Darren queried.

'Only if someone grassed me up,' said Lee. 'Even then they couldn't prove it. I wore those gloves so there'd be no fingerprints.'

'What about footprints?'

'You can't make a footprint on a carpet unless your shoes are dirty,' said Lee reassuringly, though his brother's question worried him. Could he have left footprints?

'What about DNA samples?' continued Darren.

'Darren, you watch too much TV,' said Lee. 'Come on, let's go and see if that little den we made last summer's still there.'

By the time they got home that evening, the morning's events seemed further away and less alarming. Lee was pleased to see that Dad was already out. Mum was sitting in her chair, knitting something pink.

'Did you have a nice day?' she asked.

'Yeah, it was fun,' said Darren, and settled down to watch a game show.

Chapter 7

The Jaguar

Before Lee even opened the door to the roof, he knew Ruby was there.

'Hi,' she said. 'I hoped you'd come up here tonight.'

Lee said nothing. He was unsure whether he was pleased or annoyed at her being on his roof. He did notice, with relief, that she wasn't in his little hiding place under the old door. She seemed to have made her own nest with some plastic sheeting and what looked like a ladder and a sleeping bag.

'What do you think of my look-out post?' she demanded, obviously proud of her creation.

'It should keep you dry,' he said, and climbed into his own.

Lee was suddenly aware that night had fallen. He felt a sense of relief, as if the darkness was an old friend. Then a thought struck him.

'Why did you call it a look-out post?' he asked.

59

Ruby grinned back at him. He noticed she'd hidden her bright red hair again, this time under a bright red hat.

'Because that's exactly what it is,' she said.

'What are you going to look out for, then?' he asked.

'Oh, you know – shooting stars, comets, alien spacecraft. That sort of thing.'

'You've got to be joking.'

'Why?'

'Well, you don't really expect to see alien spaceships, do you?'

'Why not?'

'Why would aliens want to come to Morden?'

'I hadn't thought of that. OK. I'll just stick to the stars and comets, then.'

Lee leaned back in his shelter and pulled the blanket up over his shoulders. He gazed up into the darkness. It was a clear night and he could see stars staring down at him. An aeroplane crossed the sky, its lights flickering. Ruby was right. It was a pretty good place for a look-out post.

Sunday mornings were always the worst times. Dad would be hung over and furious with himself for spending so much money at the pub the night before. Lee thought it best if he and Darren made themselves scarce. They always had dinner with Della on Sundays anyway – they'd just go early.

As he closed the flat door very quietly he heard his Dad calling, 'Lee! Come here!'

He and Darren turned and ran down the stairs as fast as they could. 'Just in time!' Lee panted, in the main hallway. 'We'd better go round the back so he can't call us from the balcony.'

It was about ten o'clock when they arrived at Della's house. Outside was the kind of car they only usually saw on television or speeding through the traffic. It was a shiny, new Jaguar in a pale metallic turquoise.

'Wow,' said Darren.

Lee stared at it admiringly, then realised that the front window was open and he knew the man sitting in the car. He was the driver for a very rich man called Leslie Potts, who visited Della regularly for consultations.

'Hello, Mr Watson,' said Lee.

'Hello, young man,' smiled Mr Watson.

'When did he get the new car?' asked Lee, stroking the shiny paintwork.

'Only last week. The other one were two year old. 'E won't have a car beyond two year.'

'How much is a car like this?'

'God knows. I don't buy 'em. I just drive 'em. More 'n you'll ever earn, I expect.'

'Is it nice to drive?'

'It's a dream.'

Darren was stroking the little silver jaguar on the front of the car.

'No grubby finger marks, young Darren!' Mr Watson stared at the boys for a couple of minutes. 'Are you clean?' he asked.

'What d'you mean?'

'Hands, shoes, clothes. Are you clean?'

'Yeah, I think so,' replied Lee.

'Well, go on. Hop in. I'll just take you round the block. His nibs will be a while longer an' 'e won't mind.'

The boys needed no further invitation. They jumped on to the back seat and examined everything – the soft leather seats, the lights, the compartments and pockets. Mr Watson put the radio on and they examined the speakers. They hardly really noticed the car was moving, it was so quiet. They turned their attention to the panel in front of Mr Watson, full of dials and lights and indicators. He demonstrated the sound control, the air conditioning, the light control and all the automatic dials. It was beautiful.

Lee leaned back in the soft leather and gazed out of the window. What must it be like to be rich enough to have a car like this and your own driver? What must it be like to just escape from these city streets whenever you felt like it? As they drove along they saw people looking admiringly or enviously, or both, at the car. Some were people they knew. As they turned the corner into the main road Lee saw Yaz and his mates with a group of girls standing on the corner. Lee ducked and pulled Darren down with him. He could hear them hurling abuse in the direction of the car.

'Haven't they got 'aught better to do?' sighed Mr Watson.

'Did they see us?' whispered Lee.

'I doubt it, lad. Anyhow, you can sit up again now.'

Mr Watson drove them back to Della's house. The boys hung around talking to him for a while until his boss came out.

Leslie Potts was a flashy man. He was wearing a shiny, expensive-looking suit and a lot of gold jewellery.

'Hello, boys. What d'you think of the new motor?'

'It's great,' said Darren, lovingly stroking the jaguar on the front again.

'I had to wait months to get this. I could have got a silver one quicker but I like the turquoise.'

'It matches your shirt, Leslie,' said Della, coming out to join them.

'It's your fault, Della,' he replied. 'You told me turquoise would be lucky for me.'

'Did I?' smiled Della. 'But Leslie, that must have been ten years ago!'

'Probably. Aren't you flattered that I remember everything you say?'

'More worried than flattered,' laughed Della.

'I'll tell you what,' said Leslie thoughtfully. 'In the spring, when I'm back from LA, I'll take you and the boys out to lunch, somewhere in the country, so you can have a run in it. Would you like that?'

They nodded enthusiastically.

'Right, that's settled. Now look after your old granny, boys.'

'That's enough of the "old granny",' Della chided.

He hugged her, solemnly shook the boys' hands and got into his sleek, turquoise car. As he drove off Lee realised Leslie had tucked a five-pound note up his sleeve and Darren's too.

'He's very generous,' said Darren.

'He is generous,' agreed Della. 'But so he should be. He doesn't come by any of that money honestly.'

'Where's it from, then?' asked Lee.

'I don't know, Lee. He's always been a wheeler-dealer, that one. I don't think I want to know what he's mixed up in. But remember, boys, if he ever asks you to work for him, say no.'

Chapter 8

Sunday

Lee always liked going to his grandmother's but he particularly liked having Sunday dinner there. Best of all was pudding. He couldn't remember his mum ever cooking a pudding but Della always produced an apple pie or a treacle tart or a strawberry trifle. Today she'd made his favourite – bread and butter pudding with little shreds of lemon peel and fat sultanas. After eating, Della said they needed some exercise to work off their meal so they went into the weak, wintry sunshine in the back garden.

Lee didn't mind helping Della in the garden. They chopped down a dead bush, trimmed an overhanging tree and cleared all the leaves that had clogged up the little pond. It was a small but pretty garden, enclosed by high walls, which made it very private. In the warm weather Della spent most of her time out there.

But that Sunday it was too cold. When they'd finished gardening, they kicked off their muddy shoes and sat in a line on the sofa, watching a soppy film. Then the boys made Della stay where she was while they went into the kitchen to make tea and bring it in on a tray.

Della never read Darren's cards. He didn't like it. He was afraid of some of them – even though she'd explained that there was nothing to be afraid of. Lee was different. He'd always loved them. He found their intricate, colourful pictures fascinating and he'd learnt from her how to interpret the pictures and the positions of the cards. Della said he had a flair for it.

Lee waited nervously for her to lay out the cards. When she had, they both stared in some surprise. In the middle, once again, was the vicious-looking circle of three swords, each held in the fist of a disembodied arm. It was a card most people would have feared, but Lee knew it was positive. He was used to the bleakest of cards, swords of a more threatening nature. This strange card he welcomed.

'Well, young man,' said Della. 'I think you've got something to tell me.'

'What d'you mean?' asked Lee.

'Who's she?' said Della, pointing to a different card that he had not yet noticed. He stared at it. It was beautiful, with none of the menace of the swords. On it was an elegant woman dressed like an old-fashioned princess in a long dress, with a crown on her flowing hair. She was holding a decorated cup in one hand and something that looked like a knife in the other. Lee had never been dealt this card before.

'Well?' said Della. 'Who is this new woman in your life?'

'Her name's Ruby,' he answered, a bit sheepishly, grateful that Darren was out of the room.

'I like the name,' said Della.

'This card, Della,' enquired Lee. 'It's a good card, isn't it?'

'Oh yes, Lee.'

'And if the card is right, I should trust her?'

'The cards are always right, Lee. It's the people who read them who are often wrong! But not this time. Yes, you should trust Ruby.'

There was a moment's silence.

'Lee, something's happened, hasn't it?' Della asked.

'Is it in the cards?' he countered.

'No, it's in your eyes. And Darren's.'

Lee had that feeling once more, of Della reading his thoughts. He opened his mouth to tell her nothing was wrong but couldn't. He blurted out the whole story of the burglary.

'What do you think they did in that house once you'd left?' she asked.

'I've tried not to think about it. I suppose they stole something. They didn't have a car so they can't have stolen lots of things.'

'Have you thought about the police?'

At this point Darren came in. He started at the suggestion.

Lee shook his head. 'They can hurt us more than the police can hurt them,' he explained.

Della looked thoughtful.

They got home quite late. Lee knew before they opened the door that Dad was in.

'Come here, you two,' he shouted, as soon as they got through the door. He was in the living room, a can of beer in his hand. 'Where've you been all day?'

'We went to Della's for dinner.'

'I thought so. I don't want you going there again.'

'But we always –' said Darren.

'Not any more.'

'Why not?' demanded Lee, knowing, even as he said it, that it was a stupid thing to say.

'Because I don't want you going there. She's a bad influence.'

Lee opened his mouth to argue but thought better of it.

'That woman's evil. She's a dirty gypsy. She's a bloody witch!'

Lee looked at his mum. She sat, her eyes glued to the television, her hands busy with the pink wool. If she had heard his remarks, she gave no sign of it.

'I know what she's up to! She gets you involved in her dangerous games, with her cards and her spells and her crystal ball.'

'She doesn't do spells and she doesn't have a crystal ball,' Lee couldn't help correcting him.

'Of course she does spells. You're just too stupid to see it. And I forgot – she doesn't use a crystal ball, does she? She uses some kind of goldfish bowl! Well, I don't care what she uses, she's not getting you involved in her witchcraft. You're to stop going there. Next Sunday, we'll all have dinner here!'

There was no point in arguing. It was best just to wait for him to finish. He hadn't yet.

'I know what you're like, Lee. You get your slyness from your mother. I won't have you going to Della's.'

Lee said nothing.

'And don't sneak off without telling your mother where you're going.'

'Mum knew we were going to Della's today.'

'Don't use that tone with me!'

'What tone? I just said she knew we –'

'I know what you said,' he shouted. 'I'm not deaf. I heard you the first time. You're getting more and more cheeky!'

Lee took a deep breath, trying to keep calm.

'Don't sigh like that, as if you don't want to hear me. You're going to listen to me whether you like it or not.'

Lee had the urge to run but he thought Dad might just wait for him to get back. And then he'd be even angrier.

'I know what you did this morning, you know,' he went on. 'You two ran off as soon as you heard me call. I'm not standing for that, Lee.'

Lee said nothing.

'If you do that again, you'll feel the weight of my fist. Now, get to bed. I don't want to see you again tonight.'

Lee got out of the room quickly, relieved that it hadn't been worse. A little while later he heard Dad go out. He'd be in the pub now until closing time. Lee skipped out of bed and out of the flat.

He was alone on the roof. Part of him was sorry

71

not to see Ruby but he was also pleased to have the roof to himself. It became his little kingdom once again. He walked around the edge of the building, looking down at the familiar scenes. A train streaked across in the distance. Nearer, an ambulance flashed its blue lights and wailed its siren. In the car park Lee saw a group of shadowy figures. What were they doing?

He crouched down to watch them. He usually saw gangs of boys sitting or standing around smoking, drinking and showing off in front of the girls. These weren't. They were gathered round a car. Lee thought he knew whose car it was. It was the old banger belonging to the Kosovan family upstairs. Another car drove into the car park and the gang ducked to avoid the glare of the headlights. They waited for the driver to go into the flats, then clustered round the car again. Lee watched, squinting to try and see more clearly. Suddenly they stepped back. The driver's door was swung open, the bonnet was lifted! Two of the figures leaned into the bonnet. Another sat behind the wheel. The others leaned against the boot, like sentries. Then they all moved fast. The bonnet lid was slammed down, the whole group jumped into the car and it began to move rather unsteadily across the car park. It just missed a van, just missed a caravan and then sped out of the car park and along the road. Lee watched it as far as he could, then it got lost in the traffic of the main road. He was sure he knew who was driving it.

Chapter 9

Haiku

Lee saw the car on the way to school. It was on the road that bordered the school playing fields. It was just a burnt-out hulk, only recognisable from the odd green paintwork which could still be seen on one side.

He arrived at school determined to stay. He went to his form room and sat quietly, pretending to be busy with things in his bag. There was a heated conversation going on.

'Hey,' said a boy called Ivan. 'Did you lot hear about the big fight at Yvonne's party?'

'Fight? Who was it?'

'Tony and Seb.'

'Oh no,' sighed one of the girls theatrically. 'They weren't fighting over their stupid tags, were they?'

'Course! What else would those two fight about?'

Lee knew the two boys. They were famous for their elaborate graffiti. Their tags – 'Stoner' and

74

'Sabba' – could be seen on all the local buildings and along the railway tracks. Lee didn't like Tony's spiky Stoner, but he rather admired Seb's elaborate, colourful Sabba.

'Who won, then?' demanded one of the boys.

'Tony. Julie told me Seb ended up with a bloody nose and his eye all closed up.'

'That's rubbish!' pronounced a new arrival, Anup. 'Seb gave Tony a real batting. He had him on the floor and he was kicking him. It was Tony's face that was all mash-up. Seb walked away like nothing happened.'

'How did it start?'

'Tony was taking the mick out of Seb. He said he didn't dare do his tags on anything higher than a garden wall. Then they were saying I've done this building and that building and it went on like that.'

'Stupid idiots,' said Tracey. 'What's the point of arguing over a stupid tag?'

'Well I bet you wouldn't dare put your tag on anywhere high up!'

'Like where?' demanded Tracey.

'Like … like the garage over there.'

Anup pointed out of the window. There was a garage with a flat roof and a little tower at the front, completely covered in graffiti.

'Is yours there?' countered Tracey.

'Yeah – can't you see it?'

'No. I don't know what it is!'

'It's "Puma" – look, it's black and red.'

They all crowded at the window, trying to make out Anup's Puma from the rest. Lee joined them.

'What's your tag then, Lee?' demanded Tracey.

'My tag?' repeated Lee, trying to think fast.

'You mean you haven't got one?' she continued in a mocking voice.

'I have,' said Lee.

'What is it, then?' demanded her friend.

Lee wished he hadn't got into this conversation.

'It's … it's Hite.'

'Height? How d'you spell it?'

He wasn't quite expecting this.

'H-i-t-e,' he said.

There was laughter.

'Why H-i-t-e?' continued Tracey.

'Because he thinks that's how you spell height,' yelled her friend to more laughter.

'Is that it, Lee?' sneered Tracey.

Lee tried to dig himself out of the hole he'd dug.

'No … it's just that … it's just … because I wanted

76

it to have something to do with my name, Highsmith, and with being high up, but a bit different. That's all.'

'Very clever,' said Anup sarcastically. 'But I bet you Hite doesn't reach any heights, does it?'

The others giggled.

'Where have you put your tag so far?' asked Anup's friend.

What was he to say?

'Not many places, yet.'

There was a chorus of snorts and dismissive noises.

'Is it up on the garage tower?'

'Not yet,' replied Lee.

'I bet you it never will be,' sneered Tracey.

'It will soon,' said Lee.

'I'll believe that when I see it,' continued Tracey.

'He hasn't got the guts,' added Anup.

'I don't suppose he'd be able to spell it the same way twice,' said Tracey's friend, and there was general laughter.

Lee wanted to escape but his form tutor arrived and the laughter and taunts stopped. Lee had a moment to think. Why on earth had he made up that stuff about a tag? Now he not only had to design it but he'd also have to get on to the garage roof and write it on the tower. Otherwise he'd never hear the end of it. Tracey and Anup wouldn't forget.

He'd thought about graffiti lots of times. He didn't really like the look of most of it. He thought it looked too spiky and messy. The only ones he admired were the big ones with bold letters filled in with patterns and bright colours. Like most of his classmates he'd played with various ideas for his own tag, and in his little sketchbook, hidden on the roof, were some of his early attempts at designing his own. Hite had only been one among many ideas – but now it seemed he was destined to be Hite.

Where was he going to get the paint? He remembered the five pounds Leslie Potts had given him. What colours? He'd always thought blue looked good. But he'd like to do a different colour outline. Maybe a darker blue or yellow? Not black. Everyone used black. But even if he got the paint, he'd have to practise. He'd never sprayed anything in his life. He'd have to practise somewhere that no one went to, just in case his first attempt was a disaster. On the roof at home? No, Ruby might see it and she'd laugh at him if it was really bad. It would have to be somewhere more private. Then he had an idea …

Lee had to go to ordinary lessons that day. The first was maths. He didn't mind maths. Today they started off with a mental maths test. Lee liked these. You never had to write much down and he always worked things out in his head anyway. But after that they had to do something on triangles. This was what he hated – having to draw them. His triangles never had straight sides and the lines never quite met each other in the corners. He never had a ruler or a pencil sharpener, so the lines came out fat and wobbly and ugly. He looked at his neighbour's book. Her triangles were perfectly formed with fine straight lines and neat numbers on them. He looked at his again and ripped the page out of his book.

'Lee, I've told you not to do that!' said the teacher sharply.

Lee asked the girl with the neat book if he could borrow a pencil sharpener.

'I don't have one,' she said, zipping up her fat pencil case.

He thought that things would get better during art. It was a subject he sometimes even enjoyed. But his heart sank when he went into the art room. The pretty Australian teacher who usually took them wasn't there. Instead the ferocious ICT teacher stood like some kind of general at the front of the class.

'Find your seats quickly,' he barked. 'Sit down, coats and bags away. In front of you, find a sheet of paper, a pencil and a leaf. Your task: draw the leaf carefully, using different sorts of shading. When you've finished, use your drawing and the leaf to design a ceramic tile. Any questions?'

Lee looked at the rather forlorn leaf in front of him. What he liked doing in art was painting and collage, not drawing something as detailed as a leaf, with the monster from the computer room glaring at them all.

'Are you really going to put your tag on that tower?' whispered Vivienne, the only person in the class who ever really spoke to him.

'I'll have a go,' he answered.

'Isn't it a bit dangerous?' she continued.

'Oh no. It looks easy to get on to.'

'I wouldn't dare. I hate heights.'

'Do you?' he said, surprised. 'I don't have a problem with heights.'

'Well, good luck,' she said. 'I hope you do it. It might shut them up for a while.'

It might, thought Lee, and turned his attention to where and how he could practise.

* * *

80

'Where's your homework, Lee?' bellowed Mr Vaughn that afternoon in English.

'Sorry, I forgot,' Lee stammered.

'You always forget. You can do it now. Do you remember what it was?'

Lee shuffled uncomfortably.

'You had to write a haiku, Lee.'

Lee stared blankly at his book.

'I've seen everyone else's. Now you'll have to read yours to the class at the end of the lesson.'

He went away. Lee wracked his brain to try and remember what a haiku was. He turned back in his English book. Luckily Mr Vaughn had made them all stick in a little information sheet about haikus and how to write them.

'It has to be about a bird,' whispered Vivienne.

Lee felt his hands getting sweaty and his neck tingling. What could he write? A bird! He didn't know anything about birds. He gazed out of the window. Outside he saw, as if on cue, a fat grey pigeon lifting itself off the gym roof and launching into flight.

The pigeon ... he began. Was that three syllables? *The pigeon flew* ... One more. *The pigeon flew high*.

He felt a curious sense of achievement. He'd written the first line. What now? There were only five minutes until the end of the lesson.

The pigeon flew high ... I watch him fly.

No, that was pathetic, and it wasn't enough syllables.

I looked up to watch ... That was five. He needed more.

I looked up to watch and then ... That was the right number, but what next? *And then* ... What? *He fell down dead*? Lee remembered that happening once. A pigeon had just been flying along and it just dropped right in front of him. It had been horrible. But back to this stupid haiku.

'Right, Lee,' shouted Mr Vaughn. 'You should have finished by now. Let's hear it.'

'But –' said Lee, knowing that he was blushing.

'No buts,' said Mr Vaughn. 'Read it.'

Lee took a deep breath and read very slowly.

'The pigeon flew high,
 I looked up to watch and then ...'

He paused, not knowing what to say. He pretended to be trying to read his own writing.

'Come on, don't keep us in suspense, Lee. What happened?'

Lee looked down. Vivienne's finger was pointing to something written in her rough book.

'The pigeon flew high,
I looked up to watch and then
splat, straight in my eye.'

The class erupted in laughter. Even Mr Vaughn laughed.

'I like that, Lee!' he bellowed. 'Perhaps we'll make a poet out of you.'

Lee smiled shyly at Vivienne. He felt exhilarated by the class's approval and pleasure.

'You didn't write that yourself, Highsmith,' hissed Tracey's mean little voice behind him.

Chapter 10

Hite

Lee didn't go straight home. First he went to the big bargain shop in the High Street and bought two cans of blue paint and another one of yellow.

'I hope I'm not going to see that all over my bloody wall,' said the shopkeeper.

'No, it's for my art project,' replied Lee innocently.

He shoved the cans in his pockets and made his way down a little lane to the car park. He went up to the top section and found a quiet spot. Across from the car park was a squarish white building. It was a workshop or an office of some sort, about three storeys high with a parapet wall and a green rail around the edge of the roof. But best of all, as Lee could clearly see from that angle, it had a matching green fire escape that went from ground to roof. There didn't seem to be CCTV cameras and there was no yard for dogs to roam in. He decided to wait and watch the employees leave and try and work out if there were any security guards.

He hung around for about half an hour. Five o'clock. A group of people came out of the green door. There were about six – all women. There must be more. He settled down in his corner and ate a chocolate bar. It was not until six that the doors opened again. This time about thirty people emerged, in groups, both men and women. He saw metal grids being pulled down inside all the upstairs windows. Then two men came out and pulled down metal shutters on the big downstairs windows. Finally, with a little kick of excitement, Lee saw the two men lock the main door of the building and pull down a metal shutter over it. Then they drove away in a white van.

Lee wanted to run but he made himself walk steadily so as not to attract attention. He walked down and made his way to the green and white building. First he walked round it. Then he rang the bell at the front door. When no one answered his call, he nipped briskly round to the side and climbed up the green fire escape. It was easy. Soon he was there on the wide empty roof of the white building. And at the edge, all round, was a low white parapet wall, topped by the green railings. He grinned. So much white wall to practise on.

He crouched down and looked around. No one would be able to see him here, except office workers on the top floors of the Civic Centre, but surely they would have gone home by now. He got out his cans and chose a corner. He stood back and sprayed. He was holding the can too close – it came out wet and drippy. Kneeling further away he began again, with a bold downward line, then across and another bold vertical. Soon he had written the whole of Hite in big blue letters.

It looked all right. It was readable but it wasn't very unusual or attractive. He picked up the darker blue. This was going to be trickier. What if it came out in big blobs when he wanted a clear line? He sprayed the blue on another wall. If he held it quite close and moved it fast it came out in a narrow band. Oh well, this was only a practice. Carefully he sprayed around the edges of his sky-blue word. When he'd finished, he stood back. He sighed. It looked awful. In fact it looked what it was – someone's first attempt.

For a start it wasn't joined up. All tags were joined up. He got out his rough book and looked at the ones he'd practised earlier. He found a better one, where all the letters were joined.

He tried again. It looked a mess. The cross of the

't' looked wrong. He'd do a different-shaped 't'. He had another go.

It was better. It wasn't perfect, but it was a much better shape. He had a few more attempts, then stood back and laughed. He'd covered nearly a whole wall with his new tag. From a distance, his later efforts looked pretty good. He shook the can. The blue paint had nearly run out. It was an expensive hobby. He realised he was hungry and tired and it was getting dark. Time to go home.

All was quiet at home. Mum was asleep in front of the television, her pink knitting spread over her lap. Dad was out. Darren was in their room playing on his Gameboy. Lee helped himself to bread and cheese and found some pickle to go with it. He took it into the bedroom.

'Where've you been?' asked Darren.

'Just out,' said Lee.

'You've been doing some graffiti, haven't you?' said Darren quite coolly.

'How do you know?' demanded Lee, amazed. 'You didn't follow me, did you?'

'Course not. But those cans fell out of your bag when you dumped it there.'

Lee laughed. 'That's a relief. I thought you'd been spying on me.'

'Well, tell me about it,' continued Darren.

'What's there to tell?'

'What's your tag?'

Lee got out his rough book and showed him what the final version looked like.

'It's nice. Where is it? I want to see it.'

'Nowhere yet. I've put it on a roof that no one gets to see.'

'What's the point of that?'

'I was practising, stupid.'

'Well, now you've practised, where are you going to put it?'

'On that garage tower, opposite my school.'

'But it's covered with tags. No one'll see yours.'

'I know. I've been trying to think of a way to make it stand out.'

There was a thoughtful silence.

'I've got an idea,' said Darren. 'Paint everyone else's out first.'

'Are you mad?' cried Lee. 'They'd all kill me if I got rid of their tags. I'd be found in a plastic bag somewhere in pieces.'

'I didn't think of that. But you'll have to write over

someone's. There isn't any space.'

'Well, I'll just have to be careful whose it is.'

Later, when Lee was trying to get to sleep, his head was buzzing. Vivienne kept on creeping into his mind. He often thought about girls, but he'd never dared think about him and any particular girl. Of course the boys at school were always talking about girls. Some of what they said was just exaggeration but lots of them did have girlfriends. They hung around with them. They went to each other's houses.

Lee had never considered asking a girl out, for lots of reasons. For a start he was convinced any girl would say no. Why should she say yes? He was little and weedy. He always had scruffy clothes and none of them had fancy labels. He wasn't that clever. He wasn't popular. Lots of kids laughed at him, and even if a girl said yes, where could he take her? He never got invited to parties, he never had any money to buy drink or cigarettes. He couldn't invite anyone back home with his dad.

But Vivienne was different. The others didn't speak to her either. She was very quiet and kept herself to herself. In fact he was probably the only person in the class she spoke to. She was unusual. She even looked unusual. He had no idea what her parents looked like, but she looked like a dark-skinned Chinese girl. Except that her hair wasn't straight and black like a Chinese girl's hair. She had hair like a black girl's. Thinking about it, she was very pretty. Perhaps she'd agree to meet him. But where could they go? He was about to give up on the whole idea when he suddenly thought – the cinema! A whole plan swirled around in his mind. He'd write 'Hite' on that tower to show her and the others that he could do it. Then, when he had some money, he'd ask Vivienne to the cinema. A further thought came to him. Soon the fair would be on the common. He could invite her to that.

Just as he was on the point of drifting off into sleep, Della's words came to him – 'Who is this new woman in your life?' Perhaps the lady of the cards wasn't Ruby at all. Perhaps it was Vivienne.

Chapter 11

Running

The following day at school, Lee gazed out of the form room window, wondering how to write his tag on the overcrowded tower. There was no space at all. But even as he watched, something surprising happened. A man in overalls came out of the big garage doors with a long ladder and leaned it carefully against the little tower. Then he went in and re-emerged with a huge tin of paint and a brush. Lee was entranced.

'Lee Highsmith, will you answer your name! Just because you've made it into school two days in a row doesn't mean I'll just assume you're present without you answering the register,' said his form teacher.

'Present,' said Lee, immediately turning back to the window. The man proceeded to climb the ladder and step on to the roof. He put down the paint pot and to Lee's delight began to slosh white paint all over the highly decorated tower.

'Lee, what are you grinning about?' he heard his form teacher demand.

'Nothing,' said Lee, trying to turn his attention to the classroom. He looked around. As far as he could tell, no one else had noticed the painter. He realised, with some alarm, that the teacher was still focusing on him.

'Lee, are you on this planet at all?'

'I think so.'

'Well, answer my question.'

Lee had no idea what the question was. He stared around him. No clues. No Vivienne next to him this time to help.

'Sorry, I forgot the question,' he said, feeling foolish and painfully aware of the sniggering around him.

'I asked if your parents would be present at Parents' Evening, Lee. You haven't brought the form back.'

'No, they can't come,' he said, appalled at the thought of his parents coming anywhere near the school.

'Are you sure you've given them the letter?'

'Yeah.'

'Well, since this is such an important Parents' Evening, Miss Spicer is writing to every parent who doesn't attend, to make an alternative appointment. Shall I put your name on that list, Lee?'

'No,' said Lee, rather too quickly and nervously.

'But you said your parents weren't coming.'

Lee tried to think fast.

'But ... my grandmother's coming instead,' he said, pleased to find some way out of the situation.

'Good, I'll be glad to meet her,' said the teacher, making a note in the register.

'She'll probably come on her broomstick,' muttered someone at the back.

Lee froze, wondering what was coming next.

'What was that stupid remark?' asked the teacher.

'Anup said she'd come on a broomstick,' said Tracey, giggling. 'It's because Lee's grandma's a witch.'

Lee felt himself blush ferociously. He clenched his fists in rage.

'That's a ridiculous remark,' said the form tutor, seeing Lee's discomfort. 'I don't want to hear any more remarks about people's families. They're always hurtful and usually untrue.'

Tracey and Anup stopped their loud conversation but Lee was aware of sniggers and whispers continuing around him.

The bell went and they all trooped off to their lesson.

'Does she do spells?' whispered one of the girls loudly as she went past Lee in the corridor.

'No, but she's probably got crystal balls!' her mate giggled.

'Maybe Lee has as well,' added someone else. They screeched with laughter.

Lee couldn't stand it. He changed direction and went to the Progress Room. It was locked. If he went to his lesson now, he'd be late and there'd be more stupid comments.

The Progress Room was next to the stairs. Lee glanced along the corridor. It was empty. He ran downstairs. He had only one aim – to get away, a long way away. He dashed through the gates and along the main road to his flats. Inside he climbed the stairs two at a time until he got to the top floor and then made his way to the roof. There he lay down flat on his back, legs and arms outstretched and just stared at the sky. Soon his breathlessness subsided and he began to feel calmer. There was just him and the sky.

It was a dry, windy day. He watched the clouds race across the sky. There were different shapes – big fluffy ones and tiny little streaks, the blobby ones and the ones that look like the vapour trails of planes. He saw those too and wished he could be on one, flying off to somewhere warm and isolated.

Soon he got up and went into his little hide-away. He found his sketchbook and continued with the cartoon story he'd been drawing for weeks now. But he couldn't quite get absorbed. His mind kept coming back to the same questions. Would the school phone his parents to tell them he'd disappeared? And if they did, how could he find out before he went home? He decided to arrive home at the same time as Darren, before Dad. Then his mum would warn him if they'd phoned. She said nothing when he went in. That must mean they hadn't phoned.

Mum made them some ham sandwiches and Lee was sitting watching television, munching hungrily, when Dad came home. They knew what kind of mood he was in when the door slammed loudly.

'Where's Lee?' he bellowed.

'Watching telly,' said Mum nervously.

Dad stormed into the room and switched the television off.

'You've done it again, haven't you?' he snarled.

'What?' asked Lee.

'You've bunked off school again!'

Lee felt all his insides sink. A wave of panic swept over him.

'I went in this morning,' he said, knowing how weak it sounded.

'But then you walked out again!' yelled Dad.

'I couldn't stand it!' said Lee.

'You never can, you stupid little wimp.'

'I'm not a –'

Dad's fist stopped Lee in mid-sentence. He slammed it into his chin and sent Lee sprawling backwards.

'Don't hit him, Ted!' cried Mum.

'Keep out of this!' he screamed. 'You're so bloody useless, you don't even know if he's gone to school or not. Was he here all day?'

'No,' said Mum, hoarsely.

'How would you know, you dozy cow. You wouldn't notice if he was under your feet.'

Lee saw tears in his mother's eyes and she drew back into her chair and her knitting. Dad turned to him.

'How am I going to teach you?'

Lee moved back but Dad stepped forwards and grabbed him. He pushed him against the wall with a forceful shove. Lee felt his head and his shoulders bang painfully against the wall. He couldn't cry out. The air had been pushed out of his lungs and he bent double trying to regain his breath. Dad grabbed his shoulder and pushed it back against the wall, forcing Lee upright.

'You do it again, Lee,' he spat, 'and you'll get this.' He pointed to the leather belt round his waist. Then he pushed Lee aside roughly and stormed into the kitchen, leaving him in a heap. Mum followed him into the kitchen and Lee could hear him yelling at her.

'Are you all right?' whispered Darren.

'I'll live,' said Lee and stood up.

'Stay in here, Lee.'

'No, I'm going.'

He opened the living-room door and belted up the corridor, past the kitchen, past his bedroom and out. As he slammed the door he heard his dad call out. He didn't care. He was out. He dashed up the stairs, through the door and on to the roof. Then, finding some unexpected strength, he dragged an old cement bag across and pushed it against the door. He hoped that anyone trying it would assume it was locked. Then he went to the edge of the roof and looked over. It was dark. He could see the lines of traffic and streetlights, the lighted windows of flats and houses and shops. Below he thought he saw Dad come belting out of the front door and wander aimlessly around looking for him. He began to wonder, guiltily, if Dad had given Darren and Mum a hard time when he'd run off. But he couldn't stay. He wouldn't stay.

'What happened?' said a voice nearby which made Lee jump. 'Don't be scared. It's me, Ruby.'

Lee breathed once more.

'You startled me,' he said.

'That's nothing to what you did to me just now. You charged up here like a raging bull and then started dragging stuff about.'

'Sorry, I didn't think about you being here.'

'It doesn't matter. Why were you in such a panic?'

'My dad,' said Lee.

'Has he been giving you a hiding?' asked Ruby.

'No ...' Lee began. He looked across at Ruby. All he could see in the near darkness were her eyes, gazing at him with concern. He thought of the cards and Della's words.

'Yeah,' he said.

'Was it a bad one?'

'I think so. He pushed me against the wall and punched me in the face.'

'Sounds painful.'

'It was … it is,' said Lee, wriggling his stiffening shoulder.

'Will he do it again when you go back?' asked Ruby.

'That's it,' said Lee. 'I'm not going back. I can't stand it.'

'But you can't live on the roof, Lee!' said Ruby.

'I know.'

'Where can you go then?'

'I don't know. If I go to my nan's, he'll probably come and drag me home.'

'Perhaps you could phone Childline or something.'

'What for? I don't want social workers and people messing with my family.'

'OK, what's the alternative?'

'I don't know.'

Lee was quiet, thinking. He leaned over the roof edge once more. He saw his dad walk across the car park and down towards his local pub.

'I've got something important to do,' he said decisively, and went to drag the cement bag away from the door.

'Do you need any help?' asked Ruby.

'No, thanks. I need to do this on my own.'

Chapter 12

Yaz

Lee ran all the way to the garage opposite the school. He arrived breathless and nervous. He had studied the building carefully from various classrooms in school. He knew that the yard was well locked and that there was a CCTV camera over the doors to the yard. It didn't worry him. He'd seen a different approach. There was a row of shops with flats above them right next to the garage. The doors of the flats were on a long open corridor at the back.

Lee climbed briskly up the staircase and up to the second floor, then walked purposefully along the open corridor. At the far end, the flats joined on to the garage. He leaned over the rail and saw the wide flat expanse of roof a few feet below. He checked no one was looking, then climbed nimbly over the rail and down on to the roof. He went over to the little tower, half crouching to avoid being seen. To his delight, the painter had completed his job. It was all painted white with no sign of the hundreds of tags that had decorated it that morning.

Lee took out his can of sky-blue paint. With great care and concentration he wrote HITE on the side most clearly seen from the form-room window. He then outlined the word very neatly, first in the dark blue and then with yellow. He stood back. It was huge and quite professional-looking. Feeling a bit flushed with his own success, he added a star on the 'i', just to make it more unusual. Then he lay down on the cold, damp roof and looked at it and smiled. He would go into school tomorrow, he thought, just to see if they noticed and what they would say.

He heard a police siren wail and crept further into the shadows. When it had gone, he edged towards the rail and peeped over. Two women were chatting. He sat down to wait. They had a lot to talk about and he became impatient and cold. But eventually they moved and he pulled himself up and over the rail and on to the landing. He walked along, trying once more to look purposeful. He met no one until he got to the stairs, where two girls were coming up giggling. He recognised one of them. Her name was Tina.

'Hello, Lee, what're you doing here?' she asked.

'I was just … uh … looking for someone,' said Lee.

'Who? Was it me?' giggled Tina, nudging her friend.

'No, it's a friend of my mum's.'

'Who?' demanded Tina. 'I know everyone in these flats.'

Lee was trying to think fast. What if he said the name of someone who really did live there?

'Her name's Ruby. Mum thought she lived in one of these flats.'

'Ruby?' mused Tina. 'I know someone called Ruby but she don't live here.'

'Oh well, never mind,' said Lee and started to move away as quickly as he could.

'Bye then, Lee,' giggled Tina's friend.

'Bye,' said Lee.

'I reckon he fancies you,' he heard her saying to Tina.

'What, that little toe rag?' squeaked Tina in a tone of disgust.

Lee went on his way, his sense of achievement a little dented. He didn't go to Della's. He just went home. He was watchful, in case he met Dad, and was relieved when he reached the front door of Rockwell House.

'Well, if it isn't our little friend Lee,' said a voice he recognised.

Out of the lift came Yaz, Wilko and Ty.

'Hello, Yaz,' said Lee, making for the stairs.

'Hang on, my friend,' said Yaz, and Lee sensed the gang positioning themselves around him. He stood on the bottom step and turned.

'You were so helpful to us the other day that we wanted to thank you in person, so it's lucky we bumped into you.'

'That's nice of you,' said Lee, trying desperately to look and sound casual.

'And as a token of our appreciation we wanted to take you out somewhere.'

'Thanks, but I'd best get home. They'll be expecting me.'

'Oh, I get it,' said Yaz. 'You don't want to go out with the likes of us!'

'I don't think we're upmarket enough for young Lee,' said Wilko.

Lee knew something nasty was going on but he couldn't quite work out what it was.

'Well,' said Yaz. 'He only goes out with people who've got fancy cars …'

'And chauffeurs!' added Wilko.

Light dawned on Lee. He remembered the trip in Leslie Potts's new Jaguar.

'Well,' said Yaz. 'Will you come for a ride in my fancy car, Lee? It's not a Jag, but it's got a powerful engine, alloy wheels, air conditioning, CD player. What d'you think?'

'I'd better not,' said Lee. 'I'd –'

'He's very picky, Yaz,' chipped in Wilko. 'Don't worry, Lee, you won't be letting your standards drop. Yaz has got a chauffeur, you know. It's me. I just forgot the uniform today.'

They all grinned.

'I won't take no for an answer, Lee,' said Yaz, and looked at his watch. 'Come on, we're wasting time.'

Lee felt himself being elbowed down the stairs and out of the doors. Outside he was taken to a sporty-looking car and was pushed in the back seat, Ty on one side, Yaz on the other. As soon as he was in the car Wilko jammed it into gear and set off with a screech of tyres. No one spoke. Even if they had, it would have been impossible to hear them, the music was so loud. They soon drove into roads Lee didn't recognise. They stopped down a deserted cul-de-sac. Wilko turned off the music and he and Ty got out of the car.

'Are we there?' asked Lee.

'Not yet,' said Yaz.

Lee watched as they opened the boot and fiddled with something at the back. When they came round to the front he realised they were attaching new number plates. Soon, but without the music now, they moved on. He realised they were in Wimbledon, where the roads were wider and there were more trees and gardens. The houses were big detached mansions in white or red brick with two gates and gravel drives. They also had security lights and prominent burglar alarms.

They turned into a narrower road, bordered by gardens, then up an unlit lane. Wilko switched off the headlights and drove slowly up the lane. At the end Ty jumped out and pulled open some gates. They drove through them and into a grassy open space, which Lee thought must be a park or playing field. At the far side, Wilko stopped the car and everyone got out. They stood silently, watching and listening, but there was no sound. They were alongside a high fence. Ty led them to a gate set into the fence and held a torch while Wilko worked on the lock with a narrow-bladed knife and a screwdriver. When it was open they went through into a huge garden, full of the ghostly shadows of trees and bushes. Ty led them around the edge of the lawn.

Suddenly a shadow darted in front of them. Lee's heart skipped a beat, until he realised it was a cat. They went right up to the house and then down a pathway between the house and the garage. There was a door at the end which must lead to the front garden.

'OK, Lee,' said Yaz. 'Wilko will tell you what to do.'

Wilko pointed to a small window next to them, which was not quite closed.

'That's a toilet, Lee. Get through, then go to the back door and open it. The keys are hanging on a hook just over the kettle. There's a silver key and one that looks like a pencil. That works the locks at the top and bottom.'

'But what about the burglar alarm?'

'It's not connected. That's why we're here.'

'What if someone's in?'

'No one's in. We know where they are. Stop worrying.'

Lee wanted to run ... to run anywhere at all, but he couldn't. There wasn't any way out of this.

'Make sure there's nothing in your pockets you might drop,' said Wilko.

Lee checked.

'Come on,' said Yaz. 'Now.'

Lee put on gloves and then Ty lifted him up on to Wilko's back. From there he could reach the little window. He released the catch and pulled it open. He pushed his head through the window. Ty passed him a torch. He realised he was likely to fall straight into the toilet if he came through the window headfirst. So he persuaded Wilko and Ty to lift him right up between them so he could slide in feet first. It was quite easy.

He opened the toilet door and looked into the long hallway. All was quiet. He found the kitchen, big and gleaming and ghostly white. The keys were in exactly the place Wilko had described and he carefully unlocked the back door. The three others came in and shut the door quickly.

'Can I go now?' asked Lee.

'No, you might draw attention to yourself. Go and sit in the car.'

'No,' said Ty. 'He should stay where we can see him.'

'Right,' said Yaz. 'Just stay there. We're only going to be a couple of minutes.'

Lee stood helplessly in the kitchen. He was

convinced that at any moment the alarm would go off, the police would arrive or a key would turn in the front door. Somehow all the nervousness he'd managed to control when he climbed in and opened the door was released. His hands trembled. His legs shook. He felt light-headed and sick. He was going to fall over. He sat down in the middle of the kitchen floor, listening to Yaz and the others moving around the house. How was he going to get out of this? The fear had gone. Instead there was the blank nothingness of despair.

Yaz came into the kitchen, closely followed by the other two. Lee realised they all had backpacks.

'Come on, Lee,' said Yaz and opened the back door. They filed out and stood quietly, listening for movement next door. There was none. Ty took the lead and they crept quietly along beside the shrubs.

A sudden scraping halted them in their tracks. A door was opening behind the fence. They waited, crouching down in the flowerbed. Footsteps, then something being moved. It was a relief to hear the sound of a dustbin lid being replaced. Then the footsteps receded and the door scraped again.

Ty led them on, through the shadowy garden. At last they were out. Lee wanted to run and leap into the car. Wilko held him back.

'Slowly,' he whispered.

They got into the car, hardly daring to close the doors properly. Wilko drove slowly, quietly, across the field. When they'd gone through the gates, to Lee's surprise, Ty got out and shut them carefully. It wasn't until they got to the road that Wilko put on the lights. He drove sedately through the tree-lined streets and back to the deserted cul-de-sac. There they removed the number plates, tucking them behind an old garage wall.

It was only then that they spoke. Except they didn't actually speak. It was more a matter of making noise. Wilko put on the lights, Yaz put on the music and they opened all the windows. They roared up the little road whooping and screeching, the car vibrating to the thudding beat. Within minutes they'd reached the main road.

'Can I get out here?' Lee asked.

Yaz turned to him, as if surprised that he was there.

'Stop the car, Wilko,' he said. 'Thank you for your help, Lee. We won't forget, but I suggest you do.'

'I already have,' said Lee, and got out. 'I wish,' he muttered to himself.

Chapter 13

Smoke

On the way to school Lee's head was so full of the events of the night before that he'd almost forgotten about the garage tower. When he walked into the classroom, he realised he was the object of attention.

'Is that yours?' demanded a girl called Michelle, pointing out of the window.

He followed her pointing finger. From this angle he could see his tag, the blue glinting slightly in the winter sun. He felt a little thrill of pride. It clearly said HITE and it stood out dramatically against the clean white paintwork.

'Is it?' she insisted.

He nodded. She looked at it again, then looked at him suspiciously.

'I bet you got someone else to do it,' she said meanly.

'No I didn't,' he said, angry that she should doubt him. She said nothing more.

Several others commented on it. One boy, Rio, even clapped Lee on the back and said 'Nice one'. Finally Vivienne came in and sat down next to Lee.

'Morning,' said Lee, impatient to see her reaction.

'Morning,' she replied, studiously avoiding looking either at him or the window. Out of the corner of his eye he watched her take her books and lunch from her bag, open her locker, sort out her books for the morning's lessons, neatly pack everything else back in her locker and sit down. He pretended he was busy with his bag.

Then he noticed. Vivienne had her rough book open. On it she had written IT'S GREAT in exactly the same style as he had used to write HITE. He grinned and she gave the tiniest, quietest of smiles. Then Tracey came bouncing in and the mood in the room changed dramatically.

'Have you seen the tower?' she shouted. Without waiting for an answer she continued, 'I thought he was just having us on, but he's really done it, ain't he?'

No one really answered. Tracey looked around and spotted Lee.

'Lee!' she screamed. 'Did you really do that? It's brilliant. Are you sure it's yours?'

'I told you what my tag was last week,' said Lee.

'Course it's mine.'

Tracey started to add something but it was lost in the noise of Anup and his mates arriving.

'Look, Anup,' screeched Tracey. 'Your pathetic little tag's gone and Lee's put his up there instead.'

'What?' yelled Anup, rushing to the window. He stared in astonished silence. 'How did you do that?' he demanded angrily.

'Same way as you did, I expect,' said Lee, and there were giggles.

'But why did you paint out all the others?'

'I didn't,' said Lee. 'Didn't you see the bloke from the garage on his ladder painting it yesterday?'

Anup obviously hadn't. He stared hard out of the window, then equally hard at Lee.

'You haven't got the balls to do that,' he sneered.

'Have it your own way,' said Lee.

'Well, we've only got his word for it!' he said.

'OK,' said Tracey, unusually on Lee's side. 'If Lee didn't do it, who did?'

'Well I don't know,' said Anup uncomfortably. 'It could be anyone!'

'That's true, but it's a bit of a coincidence that it's the same tag Lee said he was going to use! Come on, Anup, give him some credit.'

Anup turned away and stared hard at the tower.

'Well, if Lee did do it, I think he's done it good,' he announced with reluctant admiration. 'But watch out, mine's going back up there soon!'

He went over to Lee.

'It's not bad,' he said, 'for a novice.' Then he added in a whisper, 'But mine'll be bigger.'

At break, Tracey rushed into the form room flushed with excitement.

'Hey, you'll never guess what I just heard down at the office,' she announced.

'Has there been a fight?' asked Michelle in a bored tone.

'No, this is about the Head,' replied Tracey.

'Don't say he's been fighting!' said Anup.

Tracey looked confused. 'No, he's been burgled.'

Lee, sitting quietly doodling in his rough book, stiffened at the word.

'I wonder what they took?' said Michelle. 'A box of exercise books and all those stripy ties I expect.'

'No, I think they took expensive stuff like his wife's jewellery and lots of CDs and things.'

'Well, I still don't think it's as exciting as a fight,' said Michelle.

'No, that's not the exciting bit,' said Tracey, relishing the attention her ownership of this news created.

'Well, come on, Trace,' boomed Michelle. 'Tell us.'

'Well, they think that it must be someone at the school who's responsible.'

'Why? It could have been anyone.'

'Because of that assembly the Head did last week,' continued Tracey, tantalisingly.

'What assembly?' demanded Michelle. 'I never take any notice of what he says in assembly.'

'Last week,' said Tracey. 'He did an assembly on celebration and stuff. He told us all that last night his family were having a big party on a boat on the river because it was his mum's 80th birthday.'

'Did he? I don't remember.'

'Well, someone did – and they did his house over while he was out.'

'But how would they know where he lived?' demanded Anup.

'They must have found out his address or seen him in his garden or something.'

'Where does he live, then?'

'In one of them big houses in Wimbledon.'

Lee's pencil slipped, leaving a huge black line across his book. It couldn't be true. It was too much of a coincidence. He felt faint. He wanted to get out of the room, but he'd probably shake too much. Anyway, that would make everyone suspicious. He must stay still and hope no one noticed his hands shaking. For once he was relieved Vivienne wasn't in the room.

'I thought you had to be a millionaire to live in one of those,' said Anup.

'Well, maybe he is!'

'Don't be stupid. Who'd work here if they were that rich? Anyway, if they think it's someone in school, what're they going to do about it? Are they going to interview us all?'

'I don't know. That woman with the red hair in the office said the police were coming in to school today.'

Lee wanted to get out of school and away from everyone. No, he wanted to be sick. Or both. What could he do? Maybe the police already knew. Maybe they were coming to arrest him. Perhaps Yaz and the others had already been picked up. What would happen if the police talked to him? Could he lie to them? Would they be able to tell if he was lying?

His instinct was to run, to put as much space as he could between him and the police. But he knew he couldn't. At least, not yet. If he left now, everyone in the class would suspect. They'd tell the police. The police would go to his house. They'd ask his dad. And then ... oh God, it was too awful to think about. Whatever he did would look suspicious. The only thing to do was keep still and try to act normally.

He picked up his pencil and tried doodling in his book but his hand was still shaking. He peered round. No one seemed to be looking. He put the pencil down and sat as still as he could.

'Hi, Lee.' A voice in his ear startled him so much, he swung round. It was Vivienne.

'Are you all right?' she said. 'You don't look right.'

Lee was overwhelmingly grateful to her. This, he thought, could be a way to explain his ... panic.

'No. I think I'm getting a cold or flu or something,' he replied. 'I feel a bit weird.'

Lee hadn't intended to tell Della any of what had happened, but as soon as she'd handed him the tea and cakes and settled into the chair opposite him, she gave him one of her all-seeing looks. He stared into his tea.

'It would be clearer, Lee, if you told me,' she said quietly, and of course he did, every detail. When he'd finished she sat quietly, her eyes half shut, her forefinger to her lips.

'Lee, none of this is your fault.'

'The police won't think that.'

'But even if they discovered that you were involved, they'd realise that the gang had forced you into it.'

'Why should they? I'd be guilty the same as them.'

'No, Lee. You're much younger.'

'But don't you see? I'd be the link! They'd think I told them about Mr Winch's party and him being out and everything.'

'But you didn't even know about it, did you?'

'Of course not. But are they going to believe that?'

Della frowned and sat silently for a moment. Lee knew what she would do next. What she always did when she was worried. She unwrapped her cards and Lee cut them. She laid them out and sighed.

'Still too many swords,' she said. 'But Lee, look at these!'

Lee gazed. He was surprised at the appearance of several cards that he did not usually see.

'I've never had Death before!' he said, slightly perturbed.

'But you know what it means, Lee. You shouldn't be afraid. Look at them all together. There will be problems but they'll strengthen you. Your thieving friends are still around, I fear, but not for ever. Your cards are full of hope.'

Lee stared at them, slightly suspicious. He did not like the figure of Death with its skeleton and long scythe. It seemed to be harvesting bodies. Its number was thirteen, which made it even more alarming. Whatever Della said and he knew himself from her years of teaching him, he could not help feeling frightened by such a gruesome card.

'Lee, you're thinking fearful thoughts. Stop! The cards only give indications. You are the one who controls your life.'

He sighed. 'That's not true,' he said. 'It always seems to be everyone except me!'

Lee felt very jumpy. Panda cars, sirens, people walking behind him or stepping out in front of him; everything made him nervous. The only place he felt safe was in the little hide-out on the roof. He'd have liked to stay there all the time but he knew he had to go to school to avoid another fight with Dad. Over the next week, he tried his best to disappear into the background at school, then he rushed home quickly to avoid meeting Yaz. At home he kept out of Dad's way and went to the roof as often as he could. As the days went by, his nervousness subsided a little and he began to resent constantly having to look over his shoulder. Why was his life so complicated?

There was only one thing in Lee's life that he felt satisfied with. That was his recent success as a graffiti artist. Walking home from school one afternoon, he realised that everyone else had painted their tags all over the place – on garden walls, in parks, subways, bus stops and shops. He'd have to do it somewhere else. Where? It seemed somehow sordid to him to crouch down beside a railway line or sneakily spray a bus stop. He wanted to be an artist, not a vandal. He would paint his name in the air – cover Morden's high places with his blue and yellow sign! Then reality hit him like a cold flannel. He'd finished the cans and had no money to buy any more.

At home, he went up to the roof. There was no Ruby. He settled down to draw his cartoons and practise his tag. But he couldn't concentrate. Something was wrong. He walked around the roof edge, looking around, then lay on the roof and gazed over the side towards Della's house. Here there were no flats, only straight rows of little houses, starting right below the flats. He stared and wondered about all the lives that were going on in those houses – eating, drinking, screaming, crying, laughing.

Then something caught his eye and snapped him out of his reverie. There was something strange about the row of houses below him. He looked more carefully. Then his heart skipped a beat. Smoke. There was smoke billowing out of the window of one of the houses. He jumped up. What should he do? He couldn't dial 999 – he didn't know the address of the house. But he knew the name of the road.

He ran down to the flat and picked up the phone.

'What's the matter?' demanded Darren.

'Sh,' said Lee, dialling 999.

'Fire!' he told the emergency operator. 'It's in York Terrace!' he almost shouted. 'I don't know the number. There's smoke coming out of the window.'

The operator asked for his name and address. Lee put the phone down.

'Is there really a fire?' demanded Darren.

'Of course there is. I'm going there – just in case no one's seen it yet.'

Lee rushed down, not noticing that Darren had followed him until they got outside.

'You'd better go back. Mum might worry,' he said.

Darren gave him the look of a much older, wiser person.

'Don't be stupid,' he said.

When they reached York Terrace, there was no one around. The smoke had been billowing out of a back window. Lee and Darren ran into the lane behind the row of houses. They saw the smoke and counted the houses in the row. It was the thirteenth house. They ran back round and banged on the front door. No answer. Lee banged again. Nothing. There was no sign of a fire engine.

'Let's try next door,' he said to Darren and pointed. Lee banged on the neighbour's door. An old Muslim man – long white beard, tunic and baggy white trousers – came to the door.

'There's a fire next door,' cried Lee.

'Is this a joke?' demanded the old man angrily.

'No – there's smoke coming out of the back window!'

The old man was obviously suspicious. He went in and slammed the door. Lee could hear him shouting to someone else in the house. Then he could hear lots of cries and shouts. They had obviously realised he was telling the truth and the door was flung open again.

Lee rushed to the other neighbour's house and did

the same. This time a young black girl opened the door a crack. It was easier to convince her because by now the Muslim family were shouting at other neighbours and beating on the door of the burning house. It was into this chaos that the fire engine arrived.

Lee and Darren stood back and watched in fascinated admiration. Firemen, looking like massive space warriors in their yellow helmets and brown overalls, leapt from the engine and within minutes had smashed down the door. Some disappeared into the house while others unreeled the long hoses. Smoke was now visible at the front windows. The firemen went in and out with bewildering speed carrying equipment. An ambulance arrived. There was now a huge crowd on the little street. No one seemed to know exactly who lived in the house. No one seemed to know if there was likely to be anyone at home. They waited, a frightened, excited crowd, nervously wondering if the firemen would bring anyone out. Suddenly there was a gasp. A fireman was seen carrying a small bundle wrapped in a blanket. Then another larger bundle.

The crowd went quiet. Lee and Darren stared in horrified curiosity. Paramedics rushed forward and the two bundles were placed on the ground. Lee was relieved to see both bundles move. Then they were whisked away into the ambulance, and the police arrived to move everyone away.

'Come on, let's go home,' said Lee. He turned away, but someone caught his arm. It was the old Muslim man.

'This is the boy,' he announced to a burly policeman. 'He warned us. If it hadn't been for him, we might all be dead!'

Chapter 14

A Name in a Notebook

The policeman looked at Lee and Darren suspiciously.

'Is this true?' he asked.

Lee shrugged.

Darren said, 'Yes, it is,' rather proudly.

Lee nudged him in the ribs.

'What's your name?'

Lee was on the point of making something up. He didn't want to give his name to the police.

'It's Lee Highsmith,' said someone.

Lee turned. It was a girl from school called Jody.

'Is that right?' asked the policeman, who now had his notebook open.

'Yeah,' said Lee.

'And how did you notice the fire?'

'I saw the smoke,' said Lee.

'How?' demanded the policeman.

'I live in the flats over there,' explained Lee. 'I saw

it from a window on the top floor.'

The policeman was noting it all down. He asked Lee's address. Meanwhile the neighbour's tiny wife had returned.

'Take this,' she whispered, and pushed something into his hand. 'It will protect you.' Then she was gone.

Lee looked around. Jody, too, had disappeared. He grabbed Darren's arm and they left York Terrace. By the time they got home it seemed a bit like a dream. Had Jody really been there? Had the tiny lady really whispered to him? Then he remembered that she had given him something. It was a screwed-up five-pound note. When he unfolded it, he found inside a strip of leather. From it hung a little blue bead with a white and black centre. He knew what it was. All the Turkish boys at school wore them. It was an evil eye, to ward off evil. He smiled and put it round his neck. He stared at the crumpled five-pound note. It didn't seem right, somehow. He kept on seeing those two little bundles. He was just about to throw the money away when he made a decision. He'd go to the hospital tomorrow and find out if they were all right. If they were, he'd keep the money. If they weren't, he would throw it away.

* * *

In the classroom the following morning, everyone was staring out of the window. Anup, as promised, had been busy on the tower. His tag was up there, PUMA – in big, bold red and black letters. And it was bigger than HITE, although Lee thought it was a bit crude and ordinary beside his own.

'What d'you think?' yelled Anup when he arrived.

There was a chorus of congratulation.

'What about you, Lee?' he demanded.

'It looks really good,' said Lee, thinking it wise to keep his artistic doubts to himself.

'Look!' said Tracey, pointing towards the window.

Two workmen were climbing on to the garage roof up two ladders. Another was standing on the balcony of the flats, where Lee had climbed down, measuring out lengths of vicious-looking razor wire.

Anup grinned. 'Well, Lee. It looks like ours will be the only tags up there. Anyone else who tries is going to get ripped to shreds unless they've got some massive wire cutters.'

'Lee,' Vivienne whispered. He turned to see her looking at him strangely.

'What's the matter?' he asked, worried that she was bored with all the graffiti talk.

'I heard you rescued someone from a fire,' she said, changing the subject.

'I just called the fire brigade.'

'Shame. There was I thinking you rushed in and carried someone out over your shoulder.'

'You're thinking of Superman.'

'Oh yeah. Does that often happen?'

'What?'

'Being mistaken for Superman.'

He grinned. 'Not that often.'

Lee went a very long route home. First he went to the hospital, which was on the other side of a big housing estate. Once he was there he didn't really know what to do. It was a huge place with dozens of signs giving the names of all the various departments and wards. How could he find out where they were? He took a deep breath and went over to the reception desk. He had to get in a queue.

'What d'you want, love?' asked an enormous middle-aged woman with the biggest pair of glasses he'd ever seen.

'I just wanted to see if someone ... two people ... are OK,' he whispered.

'Names, please,' she whispered back.

'I don't know them,' he mumbled.

She stared at him, despairingly, over the top of the huge glasses.

'Well, how am I going to find out how they are?'

Lee stared back, feeling stupid. She seemed to take pity on him.

'Look, love, if you don't know their names, how do you know they're here?'

'They were brought here in an ambulance yesterday,' he said.

'Now we're getting somewhere,' the huge woman grinned. 'Tell me a bit more.'

'There was a house fire, in York Terrace, yesterday evening. They were in the house.'

'Ah, that's what I needed. I'll just track them on the A and E lists ...' She tapped on her keyboard a few times. 'Got them!' she announced. 'They're in Burton unit. Here, use this phone and dial this number. You can ask the ward sister how they are.'

Lee hesitated.

'Go on,' she said. 'I don't let everyone use my phone!'

Lee plucked up his courage.

'Can you tell me who they are?' he asked.

'I can't give names,' she replied. 'What do you

want to know?'

'Well, it's just that one of them looked so small. I wondered … how old were they?'

'I shouldn't tell you anything,' said the receptionist, 'but I can see you're worried. According to the computer there were two girls aged seven and four. Now I'm saying nothing else. Phone up the ward.'

Lee phoned and timorously asked the nurse how the two girls were. The nurse was silent for a moment.

'Who are you?' she demanded.

'It was me that called the fire brigade,' he said.

'OK then, I think you deserve to know. They've both suffered from serious smoke inhalation but both are conscious now and comfortable.'

Lee thought that sounded good.

'What about burns?' he asked. 'Were they burnt?'

'No.' There was a pause. 'Young man, if you were the person who called the ambulance, you deserve a medal. A few minutes more and their room would have been an inferno, according to the fire service. I'm sure their mum would like to thank you. What's your name? I'll tell them you rang.'

'It doesn't matter,' said Lee. 'Thank you.' He put the phone down.

'Are they all right?' asked the receptionist.

Lee nodded. She grinned and put up her thumb. He did the same and left quickly, feeling odd.

Outside he sat on a bench to compose himself. He felt a bit weak and emotional. He knew he should be proud of himself for making the call but instead he felt, well ... humble and small. He tried to work it out. It was something to do with death being so close. For them, only a door away, a minute away, a phone call away. Life looked different after something like that.

He stood up and set off cheerfully for the main road. In his pocket he had the five-pound note and, looking up and around him, he noticed several buildings that had potential as canvases for his art. When he got to the High Street he stopped for a minute to gaze. At the end of the line of shops, in the middle of a busy one-way system, was the Civic Centre. It was the highest building for miles – twice as high as the flats to the north. He counted. It must have about fourteen or fifteen floors. It had a flat roof, in the middle of which was a smaller structure, with a curved top. There were lots of masts and aerials of one sort or another – but there was a large flat blank wall, bang in the middle. One day, he thought, one day.

He went into the bargain shop and bought some more cans of paint and wide marker pens and a couple of other things, then rushed home.

Mum was opening a tin of soup when he got home and he realised how hungry he was. Dad was out so they had a quiet tea. Afterwards he slipped out on the roof to think.

Chapter 15

Painting and Decorating

He'd hoped for some peace and quiet to make plans and do some drawing but Ruby was there.

'I came to see you specially,' she said.

'Why?' he asked, puzzled.

'I heard about you and that fire.'

'Who from?'

'I live in the next road. Everyone's talking about it.'

'Did you know the little girls?' he asked.

'No, but I've seen them.'

'Do you know their names?'

'Yes, I heard them today. They're called Anoushka and Katya.'

'What about the rest of their family? Where were they?'

'Their mum was working. She didn't have anyone to look after them and she couldn't afford a baby-sitter. I wish I'd known. I'd have looked after them. The poor woman, she's distraught.'

'But they're all right. I went to the hospital to check.'

Ruby stared at him. 'You're full of surprises.'

'So are you,' grinned Lee. 'Your hair's blue today. What happened to the red?'

'I felt like a change. Which do you prefer?'

Lee looked at her.

'Well, I think I like the red better. It suits your name.'

She laughed. 'I think you're right. The blue's not permanent, it's still red underneath.'

Lee sat down in his little shelter.

'Are you staying up here tonight?' he asked.

'Probably. Look how clear it is. It's a good night for star gazing.'

Lee gazed upwards. It was a clear, velvety-blue night. Already some stars could be seen.

'Do you know the names of the stars?' he asked.

'Some of them. It's not dark enough to see them all yet.'

'Tell me their names,' said Lee.

'Well, over there is the Orion belt. You can see two bright stars, Betelgeuse and Rigel.'

'Weird names!' said Lee, following her pointing finger.

'Well, you've heard of Gemini. That's over there. You can see the twin stars, Castor and Pollux.'

'What's that really bright one over there?' asked Lee.

'That's Capella. And over there the bright one is Algo.'

'How do you know all this?'

'I've always watched the stars, since I was six.'

'But how do you learn the names?'

'You have to look at the charts and then find the patterns in the sky.'

'What's that other bright one over there?'

'It's a planet. I think it's Jupiter, but I'm not sure. If you want to learn, I'll bring you some charts.'

'I'd like that,' said Lee. He was attracted by the beautiful names and the idea of having knowledge of something so big and mysterious.

They gazed at the stars in silence for a while, and then Lee got up.

'Something else is on your mind, isn't it?' asked Ruby.

'You're as bad as Della.'

'Female intuition,' laughed Ruby. 'Are you going to tell me?'

He really did want to tell someone and Ruby was

the most likely to understand. So he told her all about the garage tower opposite the school and about Yaz and the burglary and the police coming into school.

'Don't panic, Lee. If they could link you with the burglary, they'd have spoken to you already.'

'But what if they know it's Yaz?'

'They've still got to have proof.'

'There's plenty of that in the rucksacks. They'll try to sell the stuff they nicked somewhere.'

'Come on, Yaz has been doing this for years. He must have someone safe to sell it to. And even if they caught Yaz, that doesn't mean they'd get you.'

'Yaz isn't known for his niceness, is he? He'd grass me up.'

'Only if he got something out of it. He's not the sort to go giving information to the police, unless it would help him.'

They were silent for a while. Suddenly Ruby jumped up.

'You need cheering up, and I think I know how.'

'Don't tell me, you've got a secret island some- where that I can go and live on.'

'Not quite. I just thought you might like to do some more painting.'

'Painting?'

'Yeah. Come on, Lee. Let's paint your name somewhere else.'

'Where?'

'Up to you.'

'I'd really like to put it on the Civic Centre, but …'

'Forget it, too much security there.'

'Well, where do you suggest?'

'What about Whitburns?'

'Whitburns?'

'You know, the Whitburns factory. That big white
building across the common. I walk past it on my way
to work.'

'Work? I didn't know you worked.'

'What did you think I do?'

'I suppose I thought you were a student.'

'I was for a while but I sort of dropped out. I work
in Gothic Sounds.'

'The record shop?'

'That's the one. So I walk past Whitburns every
day.'

'Surely they'll have lots of security there?'

'It's got CCTV but I reckon they're all focused on
the doors, and I've never seen any dogs. At the side
there's a portakabin. From the roof of that, you could
get on to the roof of the front section and there's a

fire escape leading up to the main roof. It would be a piece of cake.'

Lee was about to say no but stopped himself. Why not? Why shouldn't he forget all the other things for a while and do something he wanted to do, something fun? Lee grinned. He was looking forward to his second public artwork.

'OK,' he said. 'Let's go.'

They strolled through the darkening streets. It was odd walking with Ruby. So many people seemed to know her. Every few minutes it was 'Hi Ruby', 'How's it going, Ruby?'

'How does everyone know you?' asked Lee.

'I'm not sure. I think it's because I talk a lot.'

As they approached the Whitburns factory there were fewer people. They found a bench with a good view of the building and watched. No one went in or out. Inside, dim blue lights shone in the downstairs windows.

'I'll go and bang on the door to check,' said Ruby.

'What if someone answers?' asked Lee.

'I'll say I'm looking for my boyfriend.'

It was as good an excuse as any. Lee watched Ruby go up to the front gate and ring a bell. No one came. She disappeared around the back of the building and returned on the other side. Lee joined her.

'Are you sure it's empty?' he asked.

'Yeah. Look – there's cameras there and round the back. We don't have to go near either of them.'

'But won't they have you on camera when you went to the gate?'

'No, I checked that one, too. I think some lorry's knocked it. It's facing up into the sky.'

They went round to the side. It was easy to climb on to the roof of the portakabin and from there, as Ruby had said, it was no problem to climb on to the flat roof at the top. Soon they were crouching down facing the empty wall – a white surface about two metres square.

'Shall I help or watch?' asked Ruby.

'You can help,' said Lee. He turned round. 'Do you think anyone will see us?'

'Not many people go along here at this time of night. And if they did, they'd notice that big lit-up "Whitburns" sign down there, not us.'

Lee hoped she was right. He got out his blue spray and sprayed the outline of HITE in huge letters on the wall.

'You can fill that in, if you like,' he said, handing her a can. Meanwhile he outlined the word in dark blue.

'Is that it?' said Ruby, standing back to look.

'No, we've got these as well,' he said, producing his markers.

Lee outlined the whole thing with a sharp yellow line while Ruby decorated it with an extravagant design of stars and clouds.

Then they sat and stared.

'What do you think?' he asked.

'I think it would easily win "Tag of the Year" if there was one,' she replied.

Lee, unused to being pleased with anything he did, felt a little glow of satisfaction.

'Come on,' said Ruby. 'Let's go.'

They climbed down quickly and went back to the bench. Even in the darkness they could see a big shadow on the once white wall.

'Come on. It's time you went home. You'll never get to school tomorrow.'

'Don't worry. I'm definitely going tomorrow. We're going on a trip.'

'Anywhere exciting?'

'I'm not sure. We're going on the London Eye.'

'You lucky thing. I've never been on it. You'll be able to see for miles!'

Chapter 16

The Eye

Lee managed to get the seat next to Vivienne on the coach. He loved going on coaches. He didn't really know why, except that he never went anywhere with his parents, so it always felt like an adventure.

It started off badly when Tom was sick all over the place before they'd left the High Street. Then it was a slow journey through the overcrowded streets. As they went deeper into the heart of London the buildings became higher, bigger and grander. There was a cry from everyone when the wheel of the London Eye appeared and the coach pulled up nearby. They had to go in one queue and then another, all the time watching the huge wheel with its space-age pods turning slowly and steadily.

'It doesn't stop to let people on,' said Vivienne.

'I suppose we just jump,' said Lee.

At last they were on the ramp that led to the pods.

Up close, they seemed bigger and stronger and somehow more normal. Then it was their turn. They moved through a gate and into the open door of their pod. It was just a glass egg with a bench in the middle. Lee and Vivienne stood at the far end gazing out over the churning, dirty river Thames.

The movement was almost imperceptible, but they were climbing higher and higher. They could see the workings of the wheel and the buildings across the river. Lee recognised Big Ben and was surprised at how big and elegant the Houses of Parliament were. As they moved up, more and more grand buildings came into sight. Some of them seemed familiar. He could see the bridges across the river and wondered why the water looked blue from above when close up it seemed so brown.

He was enthralled. Miles and miles of London lay around them, the buildings appearing small enough to pick up. Further down the river, an area of immensely tall, closely-packed silvery buildings caught his eye. It was their height that drew him. How many storeys must they have? And around them, like long-necked dinosaurs about to gobble them up, were cranes, dozens of cranes. Intrigued, Lee watched their necks move up and down, then swing around and dive down again. Cranes. Funny how he'd never really noticed them before.

Now they were right at the top of the wheel. To the south, in the distance, they could see the Crystal Palace tower, on top of the hill. Home must be the far side of that hill. As the pod moved down, Lee stared at the grand streets. Or rather, he stared at the roofs lining the grand streets. It seemed to him that in this crowded city you could walk for miles on those roofs, high above the noisy, busy streets. He stared hard but couldn't see a single person on any of the roofs. They were empty and inviting.

All too soon their pod reached the bottom and they had to get out. Lee stared dreamily at the big wheel until Tom was violently sick again. Lee managed to avoid getting splattered but Tracey was making a huge fuss because Tom's vomit had reached her very expensive new trainers. Lee moved away. He and Vivienne shared a bar of chocolate.

'Did you like it?' asked Vivienne.

'The chocolate or the Eye?' asked Lee.

'The Eye,' she smiled.

'It was OK,' said Lee, unwilling to expose his enthusiasm. 'I like being up high.'

'Oh yeah,' said Vivienne. 'I'd forgotten about

Hite. I suppose you want to write it on all those tall buildings.'

'No,' said Lee, genuinely horrified by the idea. 'Most of them are too nice to draw on. Anyway, no one from down in the street can actually see the top. They're too high and too close together.'

They started to follow the others. Lee was not sure where they were going until he found himself in the dark corridors of an aquarium. He didn't like dark corridors. He didn't like fish either. But Vivienne did. She thought they were beautiful. Gradually her enthusiasm and the strangeness and elegance of the fish rubbed off on Lee and he became absorbed in the dark watery world. So much so, that he didn't realise until they were in the gift shop that Tom had been taken off in an ambulance with suspected appendicitis. Lee didn't have any money to buy gifts so he stood idly flicking through a glossy guidebook.

When they were back on the coach Vivienne held something out to him.

'Give this to your brother.' In her hand was a shiny key ring with a silver shark on it.

'No,' said Lee. 'You should give that to your brother.'

'I've got another one for him. Look,' explained

Vivienne, and insisted that he take it. Lee was embarrassed.

'Thanks, Vivienne,' he stammered. 'That's … really kind.'

'It's only a key ring, Lee,' she teased.

Lee was quiet. Her thoughtfulness had touched him greatly. It made him feel clumsy and childish.

After the trip, instead of going straight home, Lee went to the library. He didn't really want to get a book out, but the library was in the Civic Centre, so he thought he might be able to discover a way to get on to the roof. Inside the building he walked past the library door and into a big reception area. He looked around him. There were a lot of people. He walked casually towards the far side of the room where he could see glass doors leading to some stairs. He was about halfway across the room when a security guard approached him.

'Can I help you, son?' he asked in a polite, businesslike manner.

'I'm looking for the children's library,' said Lee.

'You're going the wrong way. Straight back through the doors and to the left. Look, you can see it from here.'

Lee thanked him and sloped back to the library.

Inside he found a shelf of books near one of the windows into the reception area. He feigned interest in them while he studied the security outside.

'Interested in royalty?' asked a white-haired librarian.

Lee was taken aback. He hadn't even noticed what the books in front of him were about.

'Yes. I'm doing a project on ...' he glanced at a cover, '... on George III.'

'George III,' she repeated. 'This one's very good.' She pulled out a massive volume. 'You know he was completely mad, don't you?'

'Uh ... yes,' stammered Lee.

'And this one's got some good bits in as well. It's easier to read than that one.'

'Right ...' said Lee. 'Thanks.' He took the two books and started looking at one of them studiously. Fortunately the librarian went back to her desk. He gazed out of the window. There were two security guards, as far as he could see. They watched everyone carefully. Lots of people just walked past them. They must be the ones the guards recognised. Lee had seen enough. He went to put the books on George III back on the shelf but the librarian caught his eye and smiled. So he took the smaller of the two books over to the desk and presented his library card.

'You'll enjoy that one,' she smiled enthusiastically. 'If you need anything else on him, we can order it, you know.'

'Thanks,' muttered Lee.

'You should watch the film,' she continued in a confidential manner. 'It's over in the video section.'

'I'll do that another day,' said Lee, and rushed out as soon as he could. Perhaps Ruby was right. He should forget any plans to see his name at the top of the Civic Centre. It wasn't that important. There were lots of other buildings.

He was feeling cheerful as he made his way home. His head was full of the day's events. So full that he didn't notice Ty until he was right next to him.

'Yaz wants you,' he said.

'But I'm just –' began Lee.

'Now,' said Ty.

Chapter 17

A Business Opportunity

Lee found himself once more in the back of a car. Yaz and Wilko were already there.

'Hello, Lee,' said Yaz. 'How are you?'

'OK,' answered Lee.

'That's good,' said Yaz. 'That's very good. You see, I realised we hadn't really thanked you for your help the other night.'

Lee was silent, wondering where this was leading.

'You was very useful to me, Lee,' continued Yaz. 'I'll keep that in mind.'

'I think he likes you,' grinned Wilko.

'That's right, Wilks. I like Lee so much I want him to come on a little trip with me this evening.'

'But –'

'Oh dear. No buts, please.'

Lee waited, his stomach once again turning to lead.

'You see, a business opportunity has arisen and I

need your expertise.'

'What for?'

'He's very direct, isn't he?' laughed Yaz with no trace of amusement.

'You know, Lee,' said Wilko, 'that Yaz's business is of a confidential nature. He don't go giving details beforehand!'

'Nicely put, Wilko,' said Yaz, the same wolfish smile on his face. 'I give information on a strictly need-to-know basis. All you need to know is that I want you to be here at midnight tonight.'

'But –'

'There are no buts, Lee,' snarled Yaz, all trace of a smile melted from his face. 'If you don't come with us, we'll find your brother.'

Lee was silent. What could he say?

Lee went down to the car park just before midnight. A car tooted and its door swung open. Wilko started the car up and they roared through the car park and on to the main road. Soon Wilko spun rather than turned into an industrial estate and parked in the dark, deserted car park. He turned off the engine and the lights and they sat in the car.

Lee gazed around. It was a small estate with about

six warehouses or workshops of some sort. They all looked securely locked. Lee noticed they were all looking at one particular place. It was called See Dee Inc.

'Listen carefully, Lee,' said Yaz. 'You remember how you climbed on Wilko's shoulders and in through that window? Well, we just want you to do the same again.'

Lee's heart sank and he felt sick.

'Wilko's going to help you up on to that end wall. Then you can climb on to the flat roof there, and run up the slope to that bit at the top. There you'll find a small window that someone left open earlier today. Climb through it. You'll find yourself at the top of a staircase. All you've got to do is walk down two flights and open the door in front of you. It's that door there. It's one of those where you just push on the bar and it unlocks.' Yaz pointed to a door that led on to the lower roof. 'We'll be waiting outside.'

'But won't it be dark inside?'

'Wilko's got a torch for you.'

Lee looked around in panic. How could he get out of this?

'But look at that notice. It says there's CCTV, dogs and guards patrolling.'

'Well spotted!' said Yaz. 'We've thought of that. The guard and his dogs aren't due for an hour and a half. The CCTV is on the main door and the yard.'

'But there must be CCTV or alarms inside!'

'You've watched a lot of films!' said Yaz. 'Don't worry, Lee, the cameras are only in the main warehouse. There aren't any on the stairs you'll be going down. And, once we're in, Wilko here is a bit of a CCTV expert. He's going to fix that. And the reason we're going in through this route is that the alarms aren't working in this area. They had a little accident earlier today.'

Lee could think of no other questions. Yaz looked at him, then at his watch.

'Have you got it clear?' he demanded.

Lee nodded.

'Repeat it,' he ordered.

Lee did as he was told, then Yaz pushed him and Wilko and Ty out of the car.

It was cold. Lee was reminded of something.

'Gloves?' he said.

Wilko reluctantly took the big leather gloves out of his pocket and handed them to Lee, along with a torch. They reached the wall. Lee's knees felt like jelly. Just as they reached the wall a siren wailed close

150

by. All three of them ducked down instinctively.

'Ambulance,' said Ty.

Wilko braced himself by the wall.

'Ty'll lift you up. Then you get on my shoulders and on to the wall.'

Lee felt himself in a kind of trance, in someone else's world, unable to think or act for himself but simply someone else's toy. He was lifted up. He climbed on to Wilko's broad shoulders and heaved himself on to the wall. He walked along it, on to the flat roof, and viewed the sloping roof to the parapet at the top where the window and door were.

It was a long, steep slope in some kind of corrugated, delicate-looking material. Would he fall through it? He looked down. He could see the big yard, enclosed with wire-topped walls. He could see the car in the empty car park. He could see the shadowy figures of Wilko and Ty by the wall with only the tiny pin-points of orange cigarette glow to mark them out. He looked at the slope again. He'd never climb it without slipping. What had Yaz said? He said run up it. That would be the only way. He stepped back and prepared to make a run for it, his heart beating like a drum. Then he stopped and turned. What was happening?

Lee threw himself down flat on the roof. He saw Wilko and Ty run back to the car and heard the engine rev. What was this? Were they just playing some trick on him? But as he watched, he saw a white security van come screeching into the car park. Even before it stopped the doors opened and shapes leapt out. Dogs, two of them, and a guard. Then another guard. Yaz's car screeched towards the van, but it was blocking the exit. Wilko smashed the car straight into it. He must have been trying to push it out of the way. It didn't budge. The security guards were shouting and the dogs were barking wildly. Wilko reversed to the other side of the car park. But there was only one way out. The car screamed once more towards the exit and the security van. It smashed violently into it, then stopped. Lee saw all three of them jump out. The security guards were close by. It was like watching a film.

Then Lee noticed the dogs. They'd gone to the wall where he'd climbed up and were jumping up and barking viciously. They knew he was there! One of the guards began to run across. He had a torch! Lee shrank back, petrified out of his wits. He looked around. He couldn't go down, he'd be caught. He couldn't stay where he was. The dogs knew he was there and if anyone looked out of the window or opened the fire escape door they'd see him. There was only one other way. He moved, crouching, to the far end of the flat roof. From there he could jump on to the roof of the next unit. He jumped, not knowing where it was going to take him. It didn't matter so long as it was away from See Dee Inc. He ran up the sloping roof and down the other side. From here he could no longer hear the dogs or the shouting or screeching of tyres and brakes. At the end of this roof, he had to clamber up a wall, then a ladder on to a much higher one. This was a huge flat space. He rushed to the end of it and looked down. This end of the little estate was nearer to the main road and the orange streetlamps made it easier to see. Gazing down he saw that this building jutted on to yet another, then another, then another. Some were flat, some sloping, but they went on as far as he could see.

He sat back and began to breathe normally once more. The voices, cars and dogs now seemed a long way away. He was up here, up high, with just the sky above him. He was free. He leapt to his feet and almost joyfully ran across three or four more long factory roofs, only stopping when he had to climb up or down to a different level. Suddenly he came to the end of the last one. This was a low flat roof, butting on to the river. There was a tree growing beside it. Lee slipped down the tree and scrambled along the river bank until he came to a footpath and a bridge. Within a few minutes, whistling softly to himself, he arrived home.

Chapter 18

City Mountains

All seemed quiet when Lee unlocked the front door. He was just closing it softly behind him when his father stepped into the hall.

'Where the hell do you think you've been?' he demanded.

'Nowhere much,' said Lee, leaning against the front door.

'Where's that, then?'

Lee was trying to judge how much his dad'd had to drink. He wasn't slurring his words but he wasn't very sober either.

'Just out. I didn't realise it was so late.'

'I bet you've been up to no good – thieving or something, eh?'

Lee swallowed hard.

'No, Dad. I've just been hanging around.'

'Have you been drinking?'

'No.'

'Smoking?'

'No.'

Dad seemed to run out of questions. Then he appeared to grow tired of the whole thing.

'Get to bed,' he sighed wearily and stumbled into his own room.

The following day, Lee stayed at home, trying to keep a low profile. He played with Darren and helped Mum. He was a bundle of nerves. Every time the door opened, he thought it must be the police. Every time he heard cars pull up outside he expected them. He didn't want to go out in case he bumped into a policeman. Even if they weren't actually after him, he'd be so frightened they'd know he'd done something wrong. He didn't even know for sure whether they had been caught or not. Which was worse – Yaz and Wilko being caught or them getting away from the guards? Either way someone would be after him.

He was dying to find out what had happened. He wanted to ask questions, but he knew he mustn't draw attention to himself. So he stayed at home worrying, not even going to visit Della. It was a long weekend. Fortunately, he hardly saw Dad at all.

By Sunday evening, he was desperate to get out.

He slipped up to the roof. There, for the first time since Friday night, he began to breathe normally and relax. Soon Ruby joined him.

'I heard Yaz is in a lot of trouble,' she said.

'What did you hear?'

'That he was arrested.'

'Is that all? Tell me what else you heard.'

'Not much. He and Wilko were trying to do over some warehouse and they got caught.'

'Anything else?'

'Yeah. The word on the street is that they got done for assault.'

Lee felt an icy chill down his back.

'Assault? Did you hear who it was they assaulted?'

'A security guard.'

'Are you sure?'

'I can only tell you what I've heard. People are saying they pulled a knife on a security guard and he's in hospital.'

'Hospital? How bad is he? Is he going to die?'

'I don't think so. I just heard he's wounded. Why are you so desperate for details?'

Lee said nothing. He was torn between relief and horror.

Ruby looked at him. 'You were there, weren't you?'

He said nothing.

'Are you going to tell me?'

Lee nodded. He told her what had happened.

'Bastards,' she said.

'But if the police have got them, they'll get me!' said Lee.

'Not necessarily,' said Ruby.

'Why not?'

'Did anyone see you with them?'

'Not that I know of.'

'Well, that's all right, then.'

'No it's not,' cried Lee. 'The security guards will know someone else was there. The dogs were leaping up at the wall and barking. They'll ask Yaz and the others who it was.'

'So?'

'What do you mean – so?'

'I mean, they may well ask, but do you really think Yaz and Wilko are going to tell them?'

'Why shouldn't they?'

'What would be the point? If they could blame it all on you they'd do it, no question. But they'll just make themselves appear even worse if they admit to forcing a young boy into their crimes. And if you're useful to them they're hardly likely to grass you up.'

Lee was silent. It kind of made sense, but didn't calm his nerves. One fear seemed to inspire another.

'Anyway,' continued Ruby. 'How did you get away?'

Lee described his exhilarating roof walk.

'Wow,' said Ruby, her eyes wide with excitement. 'Are you going to go there again?'

'Not to the See Dee place, but I'd like to go on the roofs again. You can walk so far without touching the ground.'

'Can I come with you?' asked Ruby.

Lee grinned. 'OK, then.'

'Now?'

'Not tonight. I'm really tired.'

'Tomorrow?'

'Tomorrow.'

The following day was interminable. Ruby had not quite persuaded Lee that Yaz and Wilko would keep him out of it. He still expected to be arrested and crept cautiously along the corridors at change of lessons, jumping nervously every time classroom doors opened. When he saw two policemen by the office at lunchtime, it took every bit of determination in his body to stop himself running a mile.

He was surprised no one at school was talking about the arrests. All of them knew Yaz. He had been at the school for a while. Lee had expected someone to rush in with the latest gossip, but no one did. He was relieved to get home and started to look forward to his night walk with Ruby.

He met Ruby outside the flats and led her to the little bridge. At the other side they slipped through the railings on to the overgrown and slippery bank of the river.

Lee scrambled a little way along, alternatively ducking and reaching out for tree trunks and branches to steady himself as his feet struggled on the uneven, slippery bank. He stopped and turned. Ruby was just behind him, sure-footed and moving quietly through dense growth.

It seemed much further and much more difficult going this way. He was tired, scratched and breathless by the time he reached the tree.

'OK?' panted Lee.

'Fine,' said Ruby, seemingly unaffected by the scramble. 'Is this the tree?'

'Yeah. We need to climb up quite high. From there you can just step on to the roof.'

'Go on, then,' said Ruby. 'I'll follow.'

Lee grabbed on to the lowest of the branches and pulled himself up. He climbed steadily, sensing rather than hearing Ruby following him. It was as he remembered. The tree was close enough to slide across the parapet wall and on to the roof of the building. He reached out his hand and pulled Ruby across.

They sat for a moment to get their breath back. They were not very high up, but already the world seemed changed. The noise of the traffic was muffled. An unpeopled land lay ahead of them, and above a brilliant moon had suddenly appeared, bathing the strange rooftop landscape in a pearly, gleaming light.

'Come on,' said Lee, and began to lead the way. They strode, fearlessly confident, across flat asphalted roofs, sloping corrugation, grey tiles, pale concrete and black tar. Lee paused to show Ruby where he'd climbed up that night with Yaz.

'We mustn't go there,' she said. 'They'll be watchful at the moment.'

They turned towards an even higher building that Lee hadn't crossed before. But they couldn't get to it. It was not joined on to any of the others and there was a gap of a couple of metres in between. They turned back and returned to the tallest of the buildings they could reach. There they sat, leaning against the low wall of one of the many skylights in the roof. Ruby took out a bar of chocolate and they sat, bathed in moonlight, munching. Lee closed his eyes. He felt … yes, that was it … he felt happy.

'Thanks, Lee,' said Ruby suddenly.

'What for?'

'Bringing me here,' she answered.

'You like it, then?'

'I love it. It's like being on top of a mountain. No, a long range of mountains.'

'I suppose that's what these places are,' reflected Lee. 'City mountains.'

Lee pulled a can of blue paint from his pocket. Ruby stared at it.

'Is that why you came here tonight?' she asked.

'I suppose so,' he replied.

'Do you really want to put your tag up here?'

'You don't think I should?' asked Lee.

'Well, it might spoil it.'

Lee looked around. 'I think it'd make it look better, not worse,' he said. 'They aren't very attractive-looking buildings.'

'I didn't mean that,' said Ruby. 'I meant that it might spoil it for us.'

'How?'

'Well, if they saw your tag, they'd know someone had been up here. So they might put security cameras or razor wire or cut down the tree or something.'

Lee was quiet.

'I see what you mean,' he said at last. 'I wouldn't like it if we couldn't get up here again.'

They sat in silence for a while, relishing the peace and solitude.

'Is that Orion?'

'You're learning,' replied Ruby, and went on to point out many more stars and constellations.

Lee had no idea how long they were there. He'd probably have stayed until dawn if Ruby hadn't pulled him to his feet and insisted they go. She reminded him that he had school the next day. School. The thought filled him with dread.

'Cheer up, Lee,' said Ruby. 'Things are looking up, you know.'

'Are they?'

'Of course. That lot can't get you now they're banged up, can they?'

'I suppose there is that.'

Chapter 19

Night Walk

All was quiet when he got home. Lee slipped into bed and was soon sound asleep. He was woken, much later, by the sound of the front door crashing shut. Then he heard the familiar lurching and cussing as Dad went down the hallway. Usually, he stumbled into the bedroom or the front room and flopped unconscious on to the bed or settee. But Lee heard him in the kitchen, opening cupboards and muttering. Then he went into the bedroom.

Lee snuggled down into his bed, expecting to hear no more from his dad. But soon he was wide awake and tense with apprehension. He could hear his dad shouting at Mum and the loud sobs of Mum weeping helplessly. He wished once again that he was bigger and stronger, strong enough to keep Dad away from Mum.

The shouting got louder. He was calling her all the names under the sun. He heard them move into the living room. Then Lee sat bolt upright as he heard a crash and his mother let out a piercing scream. He didn't stop to think. He ran to the living room and rushed in. Mum was on the floor, crouched against the wall, holding her hands up to protect her face. As he arrived he saw Dad standing over her, swaying slightly but steady enough to land a fist on the side of her head. She screamed again. Neither of them had noticed Lee.

'Stop it!' he screamed, as loudly as he could. They both turned in surprise.

'Oh, who's the little hero?' mocked his dad.

'Just leave her alone, will you?' said Lee.

'What did you say?' Dad demanded menacingly.

'You heard,' said Lee.

'Get back to your room or you'll get some of this too,' his dad yelled, waving his fist in the air.

Lee stared at him defiantly, noticing that Mum had taken advantage of the distraction to edge further away from Dad and nearer the door.

'I'll kill you, you little sod,' he screamed, and began to move towards Lee.

Lee, moving fast and instinctively, pushed an armchair in his way. Dad was too drunk to react quickly and he stumbled over it, falling into a heap on the floor.

'Come on, Mum. Get out of here,' yelled Lee.

Mum, still crouching, stared in terror at the scene in front of her.

'Come on!' yelled Lee, and went to grab her by the hand. Dad was cursing and beginning to pull himself up. He had a dangerous look in his eye. Mum, like a baby, allowed herself to be helped up and out into the hall. Lee pushed the door shut behind them and led her into his and Darren's bedroom. Darren, oblivious to the drama, slept peacefully in his bunk.

'Are you all right?' asked Lee.

Mum stared at him as if he was a complete stranger. In her eyes was the wild look of a frightened animal. Lee had never seen her like this.

'Come on,' he said. 'We need to get to Della's.'

He pushed a chair in front of the door in case Dad should try to come in, but for a moment there was no sound.

'Wake up, Darren. Get dressed.'

Darren was wide-eyed and fearful. He got dressed quickly, staring in alarm at the crouching, silent form of his mum. They were ready. But just as Lee was about to move the chair, the door smashed open and the enormous form of his dad filled the doorway. Lee pushed Darren behind him. What to do? He was no match for this man. Dad started to push the broken chair out of the way to get to Lee. Lee looked around desperately.

Then, from somewhere, a new energy and thought hit him. He jumped on to the ladder of the bunk and climbed up to the top rung. As Dad lunged at him he swung his leg up and kicked him with all his strength in the side of the head. Dad tottered for a moment and then keeled over. Lee didn't wait. He told Darren to grab Mum's other hand and they led her swiftly through the hall and down the stairs. In the car park, Lee made them crouch down behind the caravan for a few minutes to see if Dad was following. They saw nothing.

Gently the two boys led their mother to Della's. It was not a long walk but it felt like the longest Lee had ever made. Della opened the door almost before they knocked. She hugged the boys and took Mum into the sitting room. Lee made sure all the doors were bolted and joined them. They sat and drank hot chocolate. Nothing was said, nothing needed saying. Della was gently stroking Mum's hair and murmuring to her.

'Up you go to bed, you two,' she said, after a while. 'You can both sleep in the big bed tonight.'

Lee looked at his mum. She looked like an empty shell.

'Should we call a doctor?' he asked Della when Darren had gone upstairs.

'It's a good idea, Lee, but not wise. Look at her. If a doctor saw her like that, he'd probably shove her in some horrible hospital full of mad people or push pills down her throat. Don't worry, I'll look after her.'

'But will she be all right again?' asked Lee, his voice quivering.

'Give her time, Lee. She's had a nasty shock and it'll take time for her to find herself again, but she'll do it.'

Lee kissed his mum gently on her forehead. She didn't react at all. He hugged Della tightly.

'Well done, Lee,' she whispered.

Despite their disrupted night, Della made the boys get up and go to school the next morning.

'But what if he comes round?' asked Lee.

'I've got a little plan,' said Della.

'What is it?'

'You'll see when you get home,' she said.

'Are you sure?'

'Positive.'

Lee took Darren to school and then went on to

his. He was in a strange state. One moment he was filled with fear and dread, especially when he thought of Mum. The next he was elated by the memory of knocking Dad down and escaping through the night. He had, after all, stood up to him at last and won. The next moment, he remembered Yaz and Wilko and the police and was filled with even more terrors. He wished he could simply clear all these thoughts from his head and be carefree for a while.

The day was uneventful. Or, at least, it seemed to be. He went through it in a daze, not noticing what he did or what was said to him.

'Lee, you seem weird again today,' said Vivienne at lunchtime. 'Are you ill?'

But he was simply waiting for the bell to go at the end of the day so that he could rush back and check everything was all right.

He arrived breathless at Della's and opened the door. He stood, rooted to the spot, as an incredibly tall young man confronted him in the narrow hallway.

'What ...?' he began.

'Hello, Lee,' said the young man.

Lee was open-mouthed. He thought he recognised him. What was happening? Where was Della? Where was Mum?

Suddenly the young man grinned.

'I'm sorry, Lee,' he said, kindly. 'I thought Della would've told you I was here, but she obviously hasn't.'

'No ...' said Lee, still staring. 'Is it you, Ty?'

'No, my name's Kyle.'

'But –'

'Don't worry, man. It's an easy mistake to make. Ty's my cousin and we do look pretty similar.'

Kyle led him into the sitting room where Mum was sitting gazing at the fire. Lee went over to her and kissed her.

'Hi, Mum,' he said cheerfully.

She turned her head slightly and looked at him. The expression on her face remained unchanged and she turned back to the fire.

'Why are you here?' demanded Lee.

'Your gran asked me to sit with your mum while she went to fetch your brother from school.'

Lee tried to get used to this freely talking, smiling young man who looked so much like Ty. How different from Yaz's silent strong man.

Kyle noticed Lee's confusion.

'I live two doors away. My mum and Della are friends.'

Lee knew about Della's friendship with Irma and he'd heard her talk about Irma's boy Kyle, but he'd never associated him with Ty.

'Was Ty arrested?' asked Lee, but the noisy arrival of Della, Darren and a dog prevented Kyle answering.

'I see you've met each other,' said Della.

'We have now,' said Kyle. 'But poor Lee was a bit surprised to see me.'

'But Lee, I told you I had plans. Kyle is one part of my plan. He and Irma are going to help me look after your mum, aren't you, Kyle?'

'Yes, ma'am,' said Kyle.

'And this.' She pointed at the dog. 'This is Buster. Darren and I have just met him. He's going to guard us, aren't you, Buster?'

Buster was a small, squarish, fluffy dog in various shades of brown.

'What sort is he?' asked Lee.

Della laughed.

'He's not got a breed. He's just a dog. Do you like him?'

Lee thought he was the silliest and sweetest dog he'd ever seen and Darren, squatting beside him, was obviously besotted.

'I'll be going now, Della,' said Kyle. 'If there's a problem give one ring on that mobile and ring off and we'll be round.'

'Thank you, my dear,' smiled Della.

Lee sat with his mum while Della and Darren were making supper. He held her hand and told her about his day at school, the other pupils in his class and his teachers. She didn't utter a word, but occasionally gazed at him with a blank, unchanging stare. He wondered, for a moment, if Della was right about not calling a doctor. He was silent for a while, thinking bleakly about the possibility that she would be like that for ever. Then to his surprise he felt a tiny pressure on his fingers. He started talking again, and his heart gave a little leap of joy.

Chapter 20

Gothic Sounds

'We need to get your clothes and things from the flat,' said Della at breakfast on the following Saturday morning. 'Any ideas?'

'Dad always goes to the pub at lunchtime if he's not working,' said Darren.

'We can just watch the building until we see him go out,' suggested Lee, who'd done it so many times before.

'OK,' said Della. 'But I don't want you there on your own. I'll ask Kyle to go with you.'

'There's no need,' said Lee.

'I'm taking no risks with you two,' she said. She slipped out of the house, returning a few minutes later with Kyle. 'Go on, then,' she said. 'Kyle, don't let them take any chances. If you don't actually see their dad leaving, don't go in.'

'OK, Della,' smiled Kyle.

They took up position behind the caravan and took

it in turns to watch the front door.

'He might already be at work,' said Darren.

'Shall we find out?' suggested Kyle.

'But he works miles away, on the Riverside Industrial Estate.'

'Well, let's phone and ask. What's the place called?'

'Snowdrop Laundry.'

Kyle phoned directory enquiries on his mobile and got the number. In no time he was phoning the laundry.

'Could I speak to Ted Highsmith, please?' he said, very official-sounding. 'I think he's working there today.' He put his hand over the phone. 'They're looking up the work rota,' he whispered. 'Yes ... are you sure? ... Monday? ... thanks ... bye.'

Kyle turned to the boys. 'Definitely not at work, so we wait a bit longer.'

It wasn't much longer. Lee watched with a kind of horrified fascination as his dad strode out of the door and across the grass in the direction of the pub. As soon as he was out of sight they rushed across. Kyle decided to wait down in the entrance hall so he could warn them if Dad came back. Lee and Darren dashed upstairs. The flat was a mess. The broken door and furniture had not been moved. There were cans, bottles and cigarette butts scattered around the living room. Lee carefully pulled out an old suitcase from under his parents' bed. He put his own clothes, some CDs and tapes and a few treasured possessions in the bottom. Darren had Della's holdall and was filling it with his clothes and treasures. Then Lee went back and started opening drawers in his parents' room. He threw underwear and tights in the case, then looked in the wardrobe and picked the clothes he thought his mum liked. He suddenly remembered shoes and put them in. In the living room he picked up a little crystal dragon that he knew she was fond of. Then he raided the bathroom.

'Have you finished?'

'Yeah,' said Darren.

'Come on, then. Let's go,' said Lee.

They stood in the hall, not moving.

'Do you think we'll ever come back here?' asked Darren.

'I hope not,' said Lee, and ushered him out.

It was nice to have their clothes and possessions at Della's. She had put a camp bed in the smaller bedroom and the boys had made it theirs. She had insisted that she would sleep with Mum in the big bed in case she woke up frightened. Lee, nervous as he was about Dad turning up, felt more relaxed there than he'd ever felt at home. But he also missed the roof. He missed the space and freedom and he wanted to see Ruby.

'You're dreaming, Lee,' said Della, coming up behind him.

'I'm missing the roof,' he said.

'And your roof companion?'

'And her.'

'Then you'd best go and see her. She'll be worrying about you.'

'But I can't go on the roof,' said Lee. 'I might bump into Dad.'

'Of course you can't, but I thought you said Ruby only went there in the evening.'

'She does.'

'It's only lunchtime. Go and find her.'

Lee thought for a moment. Della was right. He knew where she worked. He could easily go and visit her.

'I'll ask Kyle to go with you, if you like.'

'No,' said Lee. 'It's nowhere near the flat or the pub. I'll be all right.' And he was off.

Once he was on his way, he began to feel a little excited about passing the Whitburns factory. He hadn't yet seen what his tag looked like from the ground in daylight. And he wasn't disappointed. They'd painted it so high and so big, it could be seen from the other side of the common. He sat down on the bench and gazed. He couldn't believe he'd done it. It was beautiful – bright and colourful and carefully drawn. It was a big improvement on the garage tower. He wondered if any of his classmates would notice it.

Not far from Whitburns he found Gothic Sounds. It was painted black with a silver sign. Inside it was black and silver too, with lots of lights in the shape of candles.

'Lee,' cried Ruby when he walked through the door. She came up and hugged him. 'I've been worried about you. Where've you been?'

Lee stared around. There were several customers in the shop browsing through the stock or sitting on the black sofas with headphones on.

'Damian,' said Ruby to a man behind the counter with startlingly white skin and long black hair with lips to match. 'I need to talk to Lee. I'll take my lunch break now if it's all right with you.'

Damian nodded.

'Wait there a minute,' said Ruby, and dashed through a door at the back. A few moments later she emerged with a little carrier bag and led Lee out of the shop.

'I know the very place for lunch,' said Ruby.

Lee grinned. He thought he knew what she had in mind. He was right. They settled down on the bench facing the Whitburns factory and Ruby unpacked some cartons of orange juice, cheese sandwiches and grapes.

'Are you pleased with it, now you've seen it in all its daytime glory?' she asked.

'Yeah,' said Lee, through a bite of sandwich. 'I think we did it pretty well.'

'You're too modest,' said Ruby. 'It looks brilliant. It's in a league of its own.'

'I don't know about that,' Lee frowned. 'I've seen some really good ones in town.'

'OK, then. It's in a league of its own compared to most round here.'

'That's probably true,' agreed Lee.

'Now, I want to hear exactly what's been going on.'

Lee told his tale. He left nothing out. In fact it was a relief to tell someone else the full story and all the worries that went with it. Ruby listened, asking no questions and making no comment. When he'd finished there was silence for a while.

'Lee, you're a marvel.'

Lee was embarrassed.

'Don't be stupid, Ruby. I haven't done anything ...'

'Yes you have. And you should be proud of yourself.'

Lee hung his head and kicked at the grass.

'Now, I've got news,' she whispered conspiratorially.

'What about?'

'Your friends Yaz and Wilko.'

Lee felt fearful.

'They're not out again, are they?'

'Oh no. I don't think they're likely to be out for a while.'

'Why not?'

'Well, firstly they were already on probation and secondly because of the charge.'

'What is the charge?'

'It's definitely assault. I think it's GBH as well.'

'Have you heard any details?'

'The same as I told you before. They attacked the security guards and one of them was hurt.'

'And he's definitely not going to die?'

'Not according to my source.'

'Who's that?'

'The man in the café next to the police station. He

179

gets all the news. You realise what this means, Lee?'

'What?'

'It's like I said before. It means you'll be free of them. They can't force you into their crimes any more and you don't need to be looking over your shoulder all the time in case they're after you.'

They sat in silence for a while.

'Has Della got a roof for you to sit on?' asked Ruby.

Lee laughed. 'It's a tiny little house with a steep pointed roof. I don't fancy climbing on it.'

'Don't you miss it?'

'Of course I do.'

'Well, I think I might go up to the roof tonight. Do you want to join me?'

'If I could manage it without meeting my dad.'

'I could meet you in the car park and go up before you to check he's not around.'

Chapter 21

Wisps of Smoke

Della was not happy about Lee going to the roof that evening.

'I read the cards this morning, Lee. Our troubles are not over yet.'

'You didn't need cards to tell you that,' smiled Lee.

'True, but there are some other dangers. I can't say what exactly but I saw threatening strangers and a sudden shock.'

'I'll be all right, Della. I'm only going to the roof. And Ruby will be there.'

'Perhaps Kyle –'

'No, you can't ask him. It's Saturday night! Anyway, he probably wouldn't understand.'

'OK, Lee. I sense a reason for this visit. It must be so.' She sighed and hugged him. 'Be very careful.'

He met Ruby by the caravan as night was falling. She crept up the stairs ahead of him, beckoning him to follow. He noticed a light on in the flat as they went past. On the roof it was clear and bright. They watched the stars and Ruby taught him some more names. They talked of stars and music, places and people they knew, things that worried them and things they liked. They talked until they grew silent and thoughtful.

Eventually Lee said, 'It's late. I'd better get back. I know Della will worry.'

'I'll walk down first, just in case,' said Ruby.

Lee picked up his little sketchbook and shoved it inside his jacket, then looked around him.

'Don't worry,' Ruby reassured him. 'We'll find another room in the sky.'

She started down the stairs. On the floor above his flat Lee held back, waiting, while she went down to check all was clear. Then he heard her shout. Not a soft shout telling him all was clear, but a loud yell.

'Lee, come down! Quick!'

He belted down the stairs. She pointed to the front door of his flat. Curling up from underneath the door were thin grey wisps of smoke.

'Go and phone for the fire brigade,' yelled Lee.

'OK,' she said, then stopped. 'Lee, don't go in there.'

'Don't worry, Ruby,' said Lee. 'Get the fire brigade.'

She started banging on a neighbour's door. Lee found his key and pushed open the front door. Clouds of dark smoke billowed out. No one answered at the next-door flat. Ruby moved to another.

'Lee, don't!' she was shouting.

This time her banging got a response but Lee had already pulled his T-shirt over his mouth and dashed into the smoke-filled corridor. Ruby screamed as she saw him disappear and rushed to the door.

'Lee!' she cried.

Lee couldn't hear. Trying not to breathe, he'd made his way to the living room. The door was shut. He didn't hesitate. He flung it open and gusts of thick black smoke engulfed him. The smoke was not thick enough to hide the flames, which gushed in his direction as he came in. But what hit him most forcibly was the smell — a sharp, bleachy smell so strong you could almost feel it.

He spluttered and coughed and could barely see. His eyes were smarting and painful, tears clouding his sight, his nose throbbed and tingled. His lips were dry, his mouth parched and his throat felt as if he'd swallowed pins or sandpaper. Unable to see in the smoke and dark, he moved to where his dad usually slumped. He paused. He'd taken a gulp of breath. His throat burned. He could almost feel the smoke and smell filling his lungs with poison. It was like being hit inside.

Lee knew he had to get out quick. He grabbed at the chair. His dad was there. He was a big man. He knew he couldn't carry him. Staggering slightly he found his dad's feet. Turning his back to him and crouching to avoid the worst of the smoke, he grabbed one foot in each hand and made for the door, dragging Dad behind him.

When he got to the hall, he heard, as if from a great distance, Ruby's voice, and then felt her presence, coughing and wheezing beside him. Together they dragged Dad out on to the landing and shut the front door behind them. There were now lots of people there. Other people picked Dad up and hauled him downstairs. Ruby half walked, half carried Lee down the stairs and sat him on the grass outside.

He winced as he drank from a bottle of water someone handed him. Around him people, machines, vehicles were swirling in a confused unreal dance. He struggled to remember what was happening. He closed his eyes. The air seemed cold and hurt his throat.

'Are you all right, Lee?' said a gentle voice beside him.

He turned and saw Ruby, eyes wide with fear and concern. She seemed very concrete in the dreamy swirly landscape.

Then quick as a flash the mists cleared and he remembered everything. He struggled to get to his feet.

'Stay still for a while, love,' said a woman in uniform.

'But Dad!' he croaked. 'Where is he? Is he all right?'

'Your dad's in good hands. They're just taking him to hospital. Don't worry.'

Lee stared at Ruby for confirmation.

'Don't panic, Lee. He's alive.'

'Have they put the fire out?'

'Just about.'

Lee tried to take it all in. It was too much.

'I'd better get back,' he said.

'Where to?' asked the lady in uniform.

'To Della's,' said Lee.

'His grandmother,' explained Ruby. 'He and his brother and his mum have been staying there because … his mum's … not well.'

'I'll get a car,' said the policewoman.

First, Lee had to be seen by the paramedics. They

wanted him to go to the hospital but Ruby persuaded them that he was OK. In the car, the policewoman told Lee he shouldn't have gone into the flat. He should have waited for the fire brigade. Lee was only half listening. She then insisted on coming in to Della's to explain what had happened.

When she had gone, Della made Lee sip a sweet, smooth drink. She cleaned the sooty mess from his face and hands. She made tea for Ruby and they sat quietly, each grappling with conflicting thoughts.

Lee woke early, his head full of fear. He knew it had not just been a dream because he could still taste and smell the smoke and his nose and throat were sore. The coincidence of two fires frightened him. Most people probably never saw even one house fire. Was there something about him? Was he destined to be around whenever there was a fire? Was there some fire demon stalking him? He must ask the cards.

He went to see Mum. She was sitting in bed drinking tea. He sat down, took her hand and told her what had happened. She made no response. He told her he would go to the hospital to see if Dad was all right. Still no response. He went to get up and suddenly her grip tightened. She turned to him and, for the first time in days, she actually appeared to see him.

'Lee,' she whispered and squeezed his hand. Lee was ridiculously pleased. He gave her a big hug. He could see tears welling up in her eyes.

'Lee,' she whispered. 'I'm so sorry.'

Darren insisted on going to the hospital with Lee when he heard what had happened. On the way Lee talked to him about everything he could think of – except Mum and Dad. He thought he was being a good older brother until Darren said, 'Lee, stop it. You're driving me mad. We should be thinking about what to do.'

'What d'you mean?'

'You know what I mean. What are we going to do if he ... you know ... dies?'

Lee didn't know how to answer. He had had the same thought but had not allowed himself to think beyond it.

'They'll tell us what to do, won't they? People die in hospitals all the time. Anyway, Della would know.'

'But we'd have to have a funeral and all that. And Mum wouldn't be able to sort it out and we'd have to get money to pay for it all and –'

'Darren, stop worrying so much. He's probably OK.'

'That's the point! What are we going to do if he's alive?'

Lee was having great difficulty following Darren's train of thought.

'I mean if he's injured and someone's got to look after him, will we have to do it?'

'I don't think anyone can make us,' said Lee.

'Are you sure? They might send those social people to see us and they might say Mum can't look after us so we've got to go back to him or even go into some kind of home.'

Darren's voice was tearful and quivering. Lee grabbed his shoulder.

'Darren, they won't force us to go back to him. And they can't take us away, because Mum and Della can look after us.'

'But Della's getting old, Lee, and Mum isn't really ... you know ...'

'Darren, you're going to go mad if you keep doing that. Look, there's the hospital. Let's just see what's going on before we start to panic.'

Lee hoped his voice sounded adult and soothing. Inside, Darren's fears had made his stomach churn with anxiety.

To his surprise, the huge lady with the huge glasses

was at the hospital reception desk again.

'Hello,' she said. 'Have you come to see the little girls?'

'No, someone else.'

'Are you going to give me a clue this time?'

'Yes, his name's Ted Highsmith. He came in yesterday.'

'Ah yes. Is he a relative?'

'He's our dad.'

'Right. He's in Sycamore Ward, tenth floor.'

'Is he OK?' asked Darren.

'I don't know, sweetheart. I only know where you'll find him.'

They went towards the lift.

'He can't be dead,' whispered Darren. 'They don't keep dead people in wards, do they?'

'Sh,' said Lee, noticing the rather shocked expression on the face of the woman beside them.

On the tenth floor they followed a line of yellow arrows to get to Sycamore. It was not one room, it was a corridor with lots of rooms off it. They peeped through the first doors.

'Can I help you?' said a rather prickly voice behind them.

'We're looking for our dad – Ted Highsmith.'

The woman looked at a chart on the wall.

'Last door to the right,' she said, and strode away.

They peeped through the window of the last door to the right. There were about ten beds. Some had curtains round them. They couldn't see Dad but it was difficult to see the patients, what with the curtains and bandages and bedclothes that seemed to be held up on frames.

Lee pushed open the door and they went in nervously. Dad was in the last bed. He had his eyes closed. His face was puffy and one arm was bandaged. He also had one of those frames under the bedclothes. They stared. Lee wanted to go, but at that moment Dad's eyes opened and he saw them.

'Hello,' he croaked in an unrecognisable voice.

'We just came to see if you were all right,' said Lee stiffly.

Dad nodded. 'Burnt hand,' came the rasping voice. 'Burnt leg, bad throat.'

'We're glad you're ... not hurt too badly,' said Darren.

There was an awkward silence. Dad stared at them.

'We'll tell Mum that you're getting better,' said Lee. 'We should go now.'

'Wait.' Dad struggled to speak. 'Lee, they said you
... pulled me out.'

Lee nodded.

'Thanks,' said Dad, and tried to smile, though his
lips were swollen and sore.

'No problem,' said Lee. 'We'll be going now.'

The two boys quickly turned and fled, saying nothing until they were out of the building.

'Well, he's alive,' said Lee.

'Don't tell anyone,' said Darren, 'but I think I
really wanted him to be dead.'

Lee put his arm round Darren's shoulder and
squeezed.

'Come on, let's get away from here.'

191

Chapter 22

Please Go Away

Lee was astonished when he got back to Della's. He found Mum sitting at the table, laying out cards. He'd never seen her do it before.

'He's going to be all right, Mum,' said Lee.

'Good,' she replied. 'There's some biscuits in the kitchen.'

She turned back to the cards. Lee went and stood behind her, his hand on her shoulder. He gazed at the cards she'd set out. Some were familiar from his own readings. Some he had only seen a few times before. He squeezed his mother's shoulder gently. The cards were encouraging.

He was just about to go out with a big shopping list when Buster started barking wildly and Della ushered two police officers into the little sitting room. Lee recognised them both. One was the officer who'd brought him home the night before, the other was the policeman who'd taken his name on the night of the fire in York Terrace.

They sat down and looked about them. Mum stared.

'Mrs Highsmith,' said the WPC. 'Your husband is recovering.'

She looked disconcerted when Mum just nodded.

'Please continue,' said Della.

With sidelong glances at Mum, the WPC began to address Della.

'My name is WPC Wilson and this is DC Phillips. We need to ask some questions,' she said.

'Why?' asked Della with a sweet smile.

'Because of the fire.'

There was silence.

'What about the fire?'

'We need to ask Lee some questions about last night,' she went on while the other officer got out a notebook.

'Go on, then,' said Della.

'Lee,' said the WPC. 'How was it that you were at the flats?'

Lee was taken aback. He said nothing. He didn't like the silent male officer staring at him.

'He went to see a friend,' answered Della.

'A friend,' repeated the WPC, as if it was an unusual word.

'Yes, a friend,' said Della firmly.

'What friend?'

'The girl who was there last night with Lee. I'm sure you wrote her name down in your notebook.'

The WPC flicked open her notebook.

'Ruby. Is that the friend?'

Lee nodded.

'If you don't mind me saying so, Ruby is rather old to be your friend.'

Lee wanted to tell the officer that he did mind, but he felt Della willing him to silence.

'Age has nothing to do with friendship,' said Della dismissively.

'I'm not sure that's true with young people,' said WPC Wilson.

Della said nothing. There was an awkward silence. The policewoman coughed.

'Ruby doesn't live in those flats and we understand that Lee hasn't been living there for a few days, so why were the two of them there?'

Lee felt angry. He didn't want to tell these strangers about the roof.

'I needed to get something from the flat,' he said.

'I see,' continued the policewoman. 'And did you get anything from the flat?'

'Of course not,' said Lee. 'It was on fire.'

'Ah yes.' The policewoman seemed to make these two words sound sinister.

'Why do you need to ask him this?' demanded Della. 'Lee's mother is not well. Yesterday he pulled his unconscious father out of a burning flat. Can't you leave him alone?'

'Of course,' replied the woman with a toothy smile. 'We just wanted to get a few details clear.'

'What details?' asked Della.

'What time did you go to the flat, Lee?' asked the WPC.

'I don't know, whatever time the fire was.'

'That was about 10.30. And what were you doing before 10.30?'

Lee hesitated. He could see that she was trying to trip him up.

'Nothing much,' he said.

'Where were you doing nothing much?' she continued.

'I don't know,' said Lee, knowing how pathetic it sounded.

'I don't understand why you're asking all this,' said Della angrily.

'You see, Lee was seen going into the flats at 8.30.

If he was there between 8.30 and the time of the fire, he must have been there when it started.'

Della stared angrily at her.

'Are you suggesting …?'

'I'm not suggesting anything, I just want to get the details straight.'

'Lee,' said Della. 'Tell this person exactly what you did. Leave nothing out.'

Lee sighed.

'I went to the flats at 8.30 to see Ruby. I didn't go to our flat. I ran past it because I didn't want to see Dad. I did notice a light on in the hall.'

'Well, where did you go if you didn't go to your own flat?'

'The roof,' said Lee, very reluctantly.

'The roof?' repeated the WPC in disbelief.

'Yeah, the roof.'

'Why?'

'Because that's where Ruby and I meet – on the roof.'

'And what's your relationship with Ruby?'

'What do you mean?'

'Is she a secret girlfriend?'

'Don't be stupid. She's much older than me. We're just friends.'

Lee saw the woman raise an eyebrow and look at her companion.

'So you met Ruby on the roof. What did you and Ruby do on the roof?'

'Talked.'

'For two hours?'

'Yes, for two hours.'

'What about?'

'All sorts of things. And we watched the stars.'

'OK, you talk and watch stars for two hours with a girl five years older than you. What next?'

'I decided I'd better get home.'

'To the flat?'

'No, to Della's.'

'Go on.'

'Ruby went down first to make sure … Ruby went down first, then she saw the smoke and shouted to me. She went to get help and I went in and you know the rest.'

'Not quite. You tell me.'

'I went into the sitting room, found my dad in the chair and dragged him out.'

'But why did you go in?'

'To see if he was there, of course!'

'But the neighbours say he isn't usually in on a

Saturday night at that time. Is that true?'

'Yeah,' said Lee, deciding to say nothing more. They seemed to twist everything he told them to make it seem untrue. Abruptly, his mum stood up.

'Please go away,' she said quietly but firmly.

Lee stared at her in surprise. Della, quicker to recover, stood too.

'Yes,' she said. 'You've asked enough questions now. I think you should go.'

'You're probably right,' said the WPC, standing up. 'Well, I'm glad your dad's recovering. Goodbye. We'll see ourselves out.'

Lee glanced at his mum. She was gazing at the door through which the two officers had just disappeared. For a moment he thought he saw her face lit by a flash of anger. Then the moment passed. She sat back down and began to shuffle the cards.

'They think I set fire to the flat, don't they?' said Lee.

'Maybe they *are* just checking details,' soothed Della.

'No. Some nosy neighbour's told them I was there at 8.30 and they just don't believe I spent that amount of time on the roof with Ruby.'

'They may not believe you but that's neither here

nor there. They'd have to give some proof.'

'After a fire,' piped up Darren excitedly, 'they send special people to investigate how it started. I've seen it lots of times on the telly. They'll show it wasn't Lee.'

'I hope so,' said Della. 'But I don't understand why they were suspicious in the first place.'

'I do,' said Lee quietly.

Della turned anxiously. 'Tell us, then.'

'It's that horrible policeman with the notebook. He was the one who was asking me questions after that fire at York Terrace. He must think it's suspicious that I've been on the scene at two fires so soon after each other.'

'Ah,' sighed Della. 'You must be right. It must be awful to be a policeman and find everything suspicious.'

'It's worse being suspected of … of what? Do you think they're going to accuse me of starting both fires?'

'Don't panic, Lee,' said Della. 'They haven't accused you of anything yet.'

Later that day they had many visitors. Ruby came round to see how Lee was. She described how the police had asked her the same questions they'd asked Lee. Kyle and his mum came to see Della. After that, Della had several clients coming round for readings, so Lee and Darren took Buster out to the park.

Lee had grown fond of Buster and enjoyed playing with him, throwing sticks and an old ball for him to fetch. When they arrived back, Leslie Potts's Jaguar was outside and Mr Watson was sitting in it listening to the radio. They chatted for a while until Leslie came out.

'Oi,' he shouted. 'I 'ope you're not gettin' your dirty mitts on my motor.'

'Don't worry, sir,' said Mr Watson. 'I been watchin' the two of 'em like an 'awk.'

'Just as well,' grinned Leslie. 'Chin up, Lee. Things is bound to get better.'

He slid into the car and Lee found himself in possession of a crisp ten-pound note.

Chapter 23

Questions, Questions

On Monday, at school, he'd been greeted by Anup, who'd seen HITE on the wall of Whitburns.

'Lee,' he shouted when Lee got into the classroom. 'I've seen your latest. I can see it from my brother's bedroom. It's wicked, man. It's massive.'

Lee said thanks modestly.

'Did you go up there on your own, man?' demanded Anup. 'It's well high.'

'I …' hesitated Lee. 'I went on my own.'

He didn't think it was a good idea to mention Ruby. There'd be so many cheap cracks.

'You're braver than you look, mate,' said Anup.

Lee felt flushed. For three years he'd had nothing but put-downs and insults from Anup and his mates. It was difficult to adjust to this new situation where not only did Anup deign to speak to him, but he actually said something nice.

Vivienne smiled when Lee sat down next to her.

'Who's in favour, then?' she teased.

'I hope I'm not in too much favour,' Lee confided. 'I thought he was going to ask if he could come with me for a moment.'

'What a thought,' laughed Vivienne, then her expression changed. 'How's your dad?' she asked.

Lee was taken aback.

'He's all right. How did you know?'

'I've got a big family and lots of spies. Is it true you rescued him?'

Lee shrugged. 'I suppose so.'

'Superman rides again, eh?'

Lee felt the heat in his cheeks again. He looked down at his desk.

At home, he and Darren talked to Mum for a long time. It was ages since they'd talked for so long about so many things. Lee realised, guiltily, that he'd stopped talking to her properly a long time ago because she had never seemed to be listening. Now he talked. Darren talked. And she listened.

'I should have read the cards years ago,' she said, shuffling them. 'Then I'd have got you away before all this happened. I'm sorry, Lee. It should have been me, not you, that got us out of there.'

Later she laid her cards out again. Lee was astonished. They were exactly the same as the cards she'd laid out the day before. That must be pretty unusual. He told Della when they were washing up.

'Does that happen very often?' he asked.

'Only with people like your mum,' she said.

'What do you mean?' Lee demanded.

She turned to him, drying her hands.

'Your mum has a special gift, Lee. Cards come naturally to her. I never had to teach her anything.'

'But I've never seen her anywhere near them.'

'She hasn't touched them since she met … your father.'

'Do you think it's a good sign that she's reading cards again?'

'I do. Remember what I told you. She's finding herself again. That gift is one of the parts of herself that she lost. She's rediscovering that. She's rediscovering herself.'

It seemed to make sense. When Lee watched her later, shuffling and cutting and laying out her cards, she did it with a concentration that he couldn't remember her ever showing before. She'd watched television, she'd knitted, she'd occasionally made something to eat, but it had all been mechanical and she had never really been focused.

Lee went out into the little yard. It felt enclosed and restrictive but at least he could see the stars. He tried to identify the ones whose names Ruby had taught him. It was hard. They looked so similar. He wished he was on the roof of the flats with no walls around him and nothing but the sky above.

The following morning Lee was in the Progress Room with Jean. They were doing some work on spellings. It was a kind of computer game and Lee was enjoying it when the Deputy Head, Mr Winstone, came in.

'I need to take Lee away for a few minutes,' he said.

The words struck fear into Lee.

'Shall I come with him?' suggested Jean, sensing Lee's fear.

'No, no, I'll accompany him,' said Mr Winstone, even more ominously.

Lee was led downstairs to Mr Winstone's office. He knew before the door was opened who he would find inside. It was the two police officers who'd visited him after the fire.

'These two officers wanted to see you, Lee,' said

Mr Winstone, pointing to a chair.

Lee didn't sit down. He stared at the two officers.

'Why have you come here?' he blurted out.

'To see you, Lee,' said the WPC, smiling.

'Why here and not home?' he demanded suspiciously.

'No particular reason, it's just that right now you're here.'

'I don't want to be questioned here,' said Lee.

'Why not?' asked the WPC, affecting surprise.

'Because I want someone with me,' he said.

'That's why I'm here,' said Mr Winstone.

They were all sitting smiling at Lee. It felt like a trap. Lee felt a nauseous wave of panic hit his body. He dashed to the door and pulled it open. He belted along the corridor so fast he collided with someone coming round the corner. They both fell to the floor. It was Jean.

'Lee, you nearly killed me! What's the matter?'

Lee made no reply. He jumped to his feet and looked back. Mr Winstone and the two police officers were coming towards them. He started to run but found himself held fast.

'Don't run, Lee. It makes you look bad.'

'But –' said Lee desperately.

'Leave it to me,' said Jean. 'I'll talk to them.'

They stood, Jean with her arm round Lee's shoulder, and waited for the three to approach them.

'Why did you run like that?' asked Mr Winstone.

'Why d'you think, Mr Winstone? The poor lad's scared,' said Jean.

'But what of?'

'How would you feel if you were suddenly confronted with two police officers? Of course it's frightening.'

'But he needn't have run off like that,' said the WPC.

'I'm afraid Lee does have a tendency to leg it when he's upset. Isn't that true, Mr Winstone?'

'Oh ... uh ... yes, it is. Now could we go back to my office and continue this conversation off the corridor?'

Jean didn't move.

'I'm not sure that's a good idea, if you don't mind me saying so.'

'Why ever not?' asked Mr Winstone, irritated.

'Because Lee shouldn't be interviewed without his family's permission.'

Mr Winstone stared hard at Jean and Lee, then at the officers.

'I seem to have got the wrong end of the stick here,' he said angrily. 'I was led to believe these two wanted to speak to Lee about how he rescued his dad from a burning room. My impression was that they wanted to say well done.'

'They were lying,' said Lee.

'Then what is going on?' Mr Winstone demanded.

'They're trying to make out that I set fire to the flat. Go on, ask them.'

Mr Winstone looked at the police officers.

'Is this true?'

'No, not at all,' smiled the WPC. 'It's just that we have to pursue every line of inquiry.'

Mr Winstone looked like thunder.

'So you *were* going to interrogate him without his family's consent?'

'No, no, just clarify a few points.'

Mr Winstone turned to Jean and Lee.

'I'm sorry, Lee. I had no idea. Jean, take him back to his lesson. If the police wish to interview him, they can do it at home.'

Lee and Jean went up to the Progress Room.

'Thanks, Jean,' he said.

'No problem, Lee. Do you want to tell me about it?'

He shook his head.

'Not till it's over,' he said.

The police were there when he got home. Once again he had the urge to run but overcame it. Della had given them tea. Darren was at Kyle's house playing on his computer. Mum was sitting at the table, cards in her hand, staring at them.

'Come and sit down, Lee,' said Della. 'And let's get this over with.'

WPC Wilson started.

'Lee, we want you to tell us again what happened the night of the fire.'

'You know. I went into the flats at 8.30 (according to you). I went on the roof with Ruby. At 10.30 I thought I'd better go home. We saw the smoke on the landing. I opened the door; Ruby went to bang on next door's. Then I was talking to you outside.'

'When you went into the flat, what rooms did you go in?'

'Just the sitting room.'

'Why did you go there?'

'Because I knew if Dad was home at all, he'd be in there.'

'Why not the kitchen or bedroom?'

'Because it wasn't late enough for him to be in bed.'

'And in the smoke and darkness, how did you find him?'

'He's always in the same chair. I just used my hands.'

'Do we have to go through this again?' asked Della.

'I'm sorry,' came the sweetly voiced reply. 'We do need to. Now, Lee, can you tell us why you and your mum and brother came to stay here?'

Lee glanced at Mum.

'Mum was not well. Della's good at looking after people.'

'But why didn't you boys stay with Dad?'

'We … we wanted to be with Mum,' he said.

'You see,' she continued, 'we heard from neighbours that the three of you left the flat in the middle of the night.'

'That's right.'

'Why didn't your dad escort you here so late at night?'

Lee shrugged.

'We also heard that before you left there was a lot of shouting and noise from the flat. Is that true?'

'Probably,' said Lee.

'Lee,' said the WPC quietly. 'Did you have to leave because of your dad's behaviour?'

Lee didn't know what to say. He didn't want to tell these strangers anything at all. He didn't want them prying and judging.

'We decided it was time to go,' he said.

'What I'm getting at,' she went on, 'is that you weren't getting on well with your dad. Is that right?'

'I suppose so,' said Lee.

'Were you angry with him?'

Lee shrugged again. He was getting in deep.

'I think this should stop,' said Della abruptly. 'I can see where this is leading. You are suggesting that, because Lee was angry with his dad, he decided to set fire to the flat and kill him. What rubbish! Teenagers spend most of their time angry with their parents. That doesn't mean they try to kill them. If you haven't got anything more to ask him I think you'd better go.'

Lee felt proud of his feisty grandmother.

'I can understand your argument,' said the WPC, 'and we wouldn't normally have considered it a possibility, but Lee was present at a previous fire.'

Chapter 24

For Years and Years

The WPC nodded at her silent partner. He cleared his throat.

'There has been a series of house fires over recent months. Some of them were clearly accidents but others have appeared to us to be ... ah ... suspicious.'

'A series!' repeated Della. 'What are you suggesting?'

'In our investigations, we've attempted to identify common factors in these incidents,' he continued.

'And you think Lee is one of your common factors?'

'In the last two incidents, yes. It was Lee who called the fire service to the house fire in York Terrace recently. He was certainly the one who alerted the neighbours. He was there when we arrived, weren't you, Lee?'

Lee stared, unresponsive, uncomprehending. The only words he'd really taken note of were *series of house fires*. He knew now what was going to happen. He was going to be blamed, not just for those two, but how many more? And how could he prove his innocence? There was nothing he could do or say.

'That evening, Lee, you told me you were on the top floor of your flats when you saw the fire. Can you tell me what flat you were in, Lee?'

'I wasn't in any flat,' said Lee.

'That's a puzzle,' continued the officer in the same plodding way. 'Because there's no windows facing this way on the landing or staircase. So how could you have seen that fire, Lee?'

'I was on the roof.'

'The roof?'

'The roof.'

'Why?'

'I think I've explained this before. I like it on the roof.'

'Were you meeting Ruby that time?'

'No, it was just me.'

'What do you do up there on your own?'

'I draw and think.'

'But if you don't do anything wrong on the roof, why did you lie?'

'Because I don't think I'm meant to go there. And

because I wanted it to be private.'

'Private?'

'Private,' Lee repeated. 'I didn't want people to know. I didn't want anyone to find me.'

'Except Ruby.'

'Except Ruby.'

'Why is she different?'

'Because she goes there for the same reasons and …'

'And what?'

'And she can keep secrets.'

As soon as he'd said this he knew it was a mistake.

'What secrets, Lee?' asked the male officer.

Lee said nothing.

'What secrets, Lee?' demanded the officer again.

Mum abruptly pushed back her chair and stood up. Buster came and stood next to her, growling.

'Get out of here,' she said.

The two officers stared.

'I asked you to go,' Mum continued. 'Leave my son alone.'

'You heard her,' Della said, very quietly and very clearly. 'If this is how you treat people who save lives, who put themselves in danger for others, no wonder no one trusts or respects you. Now if you've got any

213

evidence that Lee's done something wrong, tell us now. If not, I'd like you to leave our home.'

They stood up.

'I'm sorry about this,' said the WPC, with her sickly smile.

'No you're not,' said Della.

'We may have to pursue this later.'

'Not without a solicitor present,' said Della, and ushered them out.

'Lee,' she said when she'd got rid of them. 'You're not to say anything to them unless I'm there. Leslie Potts said he'd get his solicitor on to it. I'll phone him now. Lee, don't you worry. Any solicitor who can keep Leslie on the right side of the prison door will have no trouble dealing with a couple of over-enthusiastic police officers.'

Lee knew Della was trying to cheer them up. He knew that she was as frightened as he was. Solicitors, police. This was a nightmare. And somehow he knew that they'd manage to link him with the burglaries he'd helped Yaz to carry out. It was hopeless.

'What do they do with criminals my age?' he asked.

'Don't even allow yourself such a thought,' said Della. She came over to Lee and took his hands. 'Lee, trust yourself and trust the cards. It will be all right, however dark it all seems now.'

Lee smiled weakly. He felt like he was trapped in a box.

'I need to get out for a while,' he said. Della nodded.

Lee wanted to see Ruby. He went up on the roof of the flats but she wasn't there. He sat for a while but it felt different. The police must have been up there – their little shelters were not quite the same. It was no longer a refuge and he felt uncomfortable there now. He went downstairs, stopping outside his old front door. It was still standing, the glass blackened by smoke. He was suddenly curious. He opened the door and stepped in.

The floor was damp and black, the walls and ceiling traced with sooty patterns. The acrid smell filled his nostrils. First he opened the broken door of his bedroom. It was untouched by fire except some darkening of the ceiling near the door. He pushed the charred door of his parents' bedroom. The fire had spread into this room. There was the blackened shell of a wardrobe and the bed was a mangled heap of wood and melted fabric of some kind. He went to the sitting room. There was no longer a door and the doorframe looked fragile. Inside was an eerie landscape of blackened debris. The ceiling seemed to have melted on to the floor and the concrete structure inside the walls was exposed. The chairs, the tables, the television had all subsided into deformed, ugly heaps on the floor. It was a miserable, depressing sight.

Lee went back to his own room and sat on his bunk to think. The more he thought, the worse it seemed. Within a few days he'd left his home and Dad, seen his mum beaten and unable to cope and seen his home burnt to pieces. That seemed enough, but added to that the police were going to accuse him of arson. They'd probably add attempted murder as well. He'd be sent away. He'd go to some prison for young offenders where he'd be with thugs like Yaz and Wilko twenty-four hours a day, seven days a week, for years and years. He'd be locked up. He wouldn't even be able to see the stars through the prison bars. It would be ... it would be torture. And who would look out for Darren? He stared around the darkening room. It was gloomy and cramped and beginning to get cold. He pulled a blanket round him.

Then, an unexpected sound. A key turned in the

lock. The front door opened, squeaking on its hinges. It slammed shut. Someone was moving slowly down the hall. The footsteps paused outside his open door, but then moved on. He heard the visitor going into the other bedroom. Things were moved. Then into the kitchen and living room. After what seemed like hours the footsteps started to move back up the hallway once more. They stopped again outside his door. Lee shrank into the corner. Then a figure appeared in the doorway. It was not dark enough to make a mistake. It was his dad. They stared at each other.

'Is that you, Lee?'

'Yeah.'

'What are you doing here?'

'What are you doing here? I thought you were in hospital.'

'Yeah, well. I couldn't stand it. I signed myself out. I don't need any treatment except clean bandages.'

'You're not going to stay here?'

'No, I just came to have a look. I'm going to stay with Arthur. He's offered me a room till they clean this lot up.'

Lee was silent. It was some time since he'd had a conversation with his dad that didn't involve shouting and threats.

'How's Mum?'

'OK.'

'The police told me she was ill.'

'That's what we told them.'

'Perhaps I'll come and see her.'

'No,' said Lee.

'She's my wife!' said Dad.

'No.'

'You're at it again, Lee,' he growled. 'Don't try to tell me what to do!'

'You can do whatever you like,' said Lee. 'So long as you stay away from Mum.'

'And who's going to stop me?'

'All of us.'

'Two young lads and a frail old gypsy. I don't think so,' he scoffed.

Lee felt something pop inside him.

'If you come anywhere near her, I'll …'

'You'll what?' sneered his dad.

'I'll kill you,' said Lee.

'Like you tried to here?' replied Dad.

Lee's heart stood still.

'What do you mean?'

'That's what the police think, isn't it? They think you tried to kill me.'

'But –'

'What do you think they do with boys who try to kill their parents, then, Lee?'

'I –'

'They lock 'em up with the scum of the earth. For years and years and years …'

'Stop it!' screamed Lee.

'And who's going to stop me seeing your mother when her murdering little boy's all locked up, eh?'

'You bastard, you bastard,' screamed Lee.

He jumped down from the bunk but his dad stood in the doorway. Lee tried to get past but Dad caught him with his unbandaged arm. Lee was desperate. He kicked out at his dad's legs. He must have hit him on the burnt side; Dad winced and clutched his leg. Lee took advantage and slipped past him, escaping from the burnt-out shell of his home. He didn't stop when he got outside. He ran, blindly. Tears ran down his cheeks, thoughts burned into his skull. He ran for miles, until he could run no more. He stopped and sank to the damp ground. He heard the clang of a can skidding across the road and opened his eyes. He tried to work out where he was. It was a patch of grass next to a narrow lane. It was rough grass, with some broken football nets. People had used the area for dumping fridges and other rubbish. Further up the lane he could see high fences and security lights and recognised where he was – on the site of the new supermarket. Something drew him to the building site. He stood at the metal gate, peering through the gaps in the wooden shuttering. They'd dug a massive square hole in the ground. There were two earth-movers. Then he saw it. It was as if this was what he'd been looking for. Nothing was going to stop him. He was going to climb the crane.

Chapter 25

Sunset

Lee didn't bother to look out for security guards or dogs or cameras. He stood back and studied the gate carefully. There were no horizontal bars to climb.

He went to the waste ground and found what he was looking for – a length of unravelling blue nylon rope. Back at the gate he flung one end of the rope over the top of the gate, then knotted it and pulled so that the rope tightened over the top of the gate. Then he took a deep breath and scrambled up the side, using the hinges as his only footholds and hauling himself on the rope. He threw the rope down the other side, swung his legs over and sat on top of the gate before jumping down into the churned-up mud.

He made his way round the huge hole in the middle and stood gazing upwards at the enormous bulk of the crane, imagining what it must be like to be at the top. He pulled himself over the tank-track base and on to the cab. From there he climbed steadily. There was no ladder; he had to stretch to reach each strut. The steel was cold beneath his hands and he was relieved when he reached the top of the section. Here, there were discs, wound with metal rope and a little light. He climbed on to the narrow strip across the top of the discs and sat down, holding on to the tall upright bars. This was the bit where the trunk of the crane joined the long arm. In front of him the arm stretched up and away, getting narrower, and from this angle looking impossibly delicate. Below him the main frame that he had climbed stretched a long, long way down.

He was out of breath but relaxed. It felt good to be so far from the ground, from life, from all those people that made his life complicated. It was even better than a roof. He could be alone with his thoughts and the sky. No one could bother him. He looked around. The sky was changing colour. Streaks of pink and orange were appearing, slashed with the darker grey of the clouds. It changed by the minute. Lee felt as if he was part of the sunset. He was right inside it. All he could see were the colours, all he could feel was the wind on his face and the cold steel in his hands.

The pink patches in the sky were getting lower.

The grey was becoming bluer and darker. Soon, thought Lee, he would be able to see the stars.

It was a sudden gust of wind that brought him back to reality. It caught him on one side and he was pushed back a little. The crane moved too. He gripped more tightly.

What was he doing up here on this metal monster? He'd wanted to escape, he realised that, and he knew it was impossible. But at least he could be alone and quiet and could think. Except that he didn't want to think – just drift with the clouds. Instead of thinking, he studied the long arm of the crane stretching away into the sky. It was narrower than the lower section and at an angle. It looked like a child's toy. And yet it picked up huge girders and bits of building. It must be strong. Somehow, the thought of climbing higher, to the end of the arm, seemed attractive.

The pink strips of sunset had left the sky now. It was velvety blue. The moon was clear. He began climbing. It was more difficult than the main trunk of the crane. It was so much higher, and since it was at an angle he faced downwards, so he was horribly aware of how high and exposed he was. Halfway along he stopped. He slipped his legs over one of the struts and sat staring into the darkening skies.

It was cold. It was beginning to get windy. It was good to feel the wind on his cheeks, in his hair, against his eyes. He thought he heard a noise. He looked down and to his horror saw a figure at the base of the crane. As he watched, it climbed on to the cab of the crane and began, steadily and unhesitatingly, to climb.

Who was it? Not a fireman or a workman – there was no yellow helmet. Who else could it be? He watched in fascination. The figure wore a dark coat and a hat and climbed fearlessly. Lee began to panic again. What could he do?

The figure was nearly at the top of the trunk section. There was a little light there. Lee waited for the face to be illuminated. Suddenly, just for a moment, he saw it, and a few minutes later, he felt the crane tremble as Ruby moved along the arm towards him.

'Ruby, what are you doing up here?'

'Oh, you know. I was just passing.'

'How did you know I was here?'

'I've been following you since you left the flats.'

'But you weren't there.'

'I was. I'd just arrived on the roof when I saw you running out the front door like a bat out of hell. So I raced down the stairs and followed you here. I was shouting to you but you couldn't hear. Then it took me ages to get over that gate. I don't know how you did it so quickly. So, here I am. Do you mind?'

'No. I'm relieved it wasn't anyone else.'

'That's not exactly a welcome.'

'Sorry.'

'Why were you running?'

'Dad.'

'Is he worse?'

'No, better. I went to the flat and he turned up while I was there.'

'What happened?'

'He said they'd lock me away for trying to kill him.'

'What? Lee, you know that's impossible.'

'Is it? The police don't seem to think so.'

'They haven't got any evidence.'

'They're the police. They can find anything they like.'

There was silence.

'Lee, I don't like seeing you so …'

'So what?'

'You know … so defeated.'

'Why not?'

'Think about it. You've got to stay strong to help your mum and Darren.'

'I've tried. I just seem to make things worse for them.'

'But they need you.'

'They'd probably be better off without me.'

'That's stupid.'

'Is it?'

'Of course it is. Come on. Look around. There's a great big world out there and an even bigger one above us. You can't let things push you under like this.'

Lee looked around at the darkened world beneath and at the vastness of the night sky. Was Ruby right? Did Darren and Mum and Della need him to be strong? He thought of his mum. She needed someone, that much was clear. In his mind's eye, he saw her laying out a cross of cards. He could see the cards clearly. They were hopeful cards. Maybe Ruby and the cards were right. Things might get better.

Suddenly a gust of wind buffeted them. They held on tight. Another followed. It was swirling around them. The crane trembled. Lee suddenly felt vulnerable.

'I don't like this wind, Lee,' said Ruby. 'It feels odd.'

'I know,' he replied. 'Let's go.'

Ruby began to edge down the arm of the crane, moving slowly backwards. A crash made them both cry out. It was thunder. Without warning a storm was upon them. Lightning split the sky, thunder vibrated through the crane. Rain came down. Not gentle drops but sheets of hard, painful, blinding rain.

'Are you all right?' yelled Ruby above the noise.

'Just about. It's difficult to keep a grip.'

Slowly, painfully, they backed down. Their feet were slipping on the wet metal, their hands ached from gripping so tightly, the fierce rain blinded them and made their skin sting. Cold, numb and frightened, they reached the lower end of the crane's arm and felt the sturdier framework of the main trunk. They paused for breath. The wind caught Lee's jacket and nearly pushed him over. Ruby grabbed at him. As she did so her foot slipped, and screaming she dropped down, clinging on with one hand, her other foot sliding on the wet metal. Lee had regained his balance. With the rain beating directly into his face and neck and chest, he moved closer to Ruby. He grabbed her flailing hand and pushed it on to the bar, holding it steady. Ruby's legs were now bicycling wildly as she tried to regain her foothold. Lee kept hold of her hand, watching fearfully. One of her feet found a solid hold, then the other. Sobbing with relief or fear or both, Ruby clung on.

'Are you OK?' Lee shouted.

He could feel her trembling violently. Or was it him?

'Just about,' panted Ruby.

'Are you ready to go on down?'

'Yeah.' She began to breathe more steadily.

Lee looked down. It was still some way to go. Another crash of thunder made the crane tremble.

'Come on, we can go down this bit together,' called Lee.

'OK then,' agreed Ruby. 'Hey, I've just thought of something.'

'What?'

'Whatever happens, Lee, it can't be much worse than being stuck up here in a thunderstorm.'

Chapter 26

Sir Ashby Something Fentiman

On the ground, Lee turned to Ruby. She stared back at him. Both of them began to laugh.

'What a sight!' she said.

'What about you?' returned Lee.

They were drenched. Everything on them dripped. Their hair was plastered to their heads. Ruby's hat had come off and her long red hair hung in heavy tails around her. Their clothes clung to their bodies. Ruby's eye make-up had formed strange black tattoos down her face. Their hands were raw, their feet were sore and now their shoes were caked in thick mud.

They laughed. They pointed at each other and teased. Lee told her she looked like a wet panda. She pushed him in the chest and he slipped and fell head first into the mud. She laughed even more hysterically and he grabbed at her legs. She slid for a moment and then slammed, bottom first, into the thick, gloopy, red mud. They sat there for a while, letting the rain beat into their faces. Above, the lightning flashed and the thunder roared. They went on laughing until their sides and stomachs hurt and they couldn't breathe. Then Ruby pulled Lee up. Slithering and sliding, they made their way across the ghostly building site and pulled themselves over the gate. They were beginning to feel cold, so they ran. Two strange, brown, mud-caked figures running wildly through the Morden streets.

Suddenly a tall dark figure, hat pulled down over his eyes, loomed in front of them. Lee stopped abruptly.

The figure pulled back his hat and grinned.

'I hardly recognised you, man,' said Kyle. 'Where you been? Mud wrestling?'

'Something like that,' said Lee, delighted that it wasn't Ty. 'Do you know Ruby?'

'We've met a couple of times, but I never seen you covered in mud before,' he grinned.

'I save it for special occasions.'

'Well, this is one,' said Kyle. 'Della sent me out to see if you was at the flat. I was just on my way there.'

'Why did she send you to look for me? Has something happened?'

'Yeah. Something good!'

'What?'

'After you left, that rich man came round, you know, the one with the Jag.'

'Leslie Potts.'

'That's the one. Well, he brought a solicitor with him. You should have seen him.'

'Were you there then?'

'Course I was. Anyway, this man was called Sir something ... what was it? Sir Ashby Something Fentiman and he had the poshest accent you've ever heard. Posher than the Queen.'

'What did he say?'

'He said you got nothing to worry about.'

'Is that all?'

'Well, that's what it came down to. Leslie Potts has had him phone the police, the fire service and everyone. He brought some papers.'

'What papers?'

'Papers from the fire people saying both fires were accidents ... and some legal papers he's given the police threatening to sue them for harassment if they speak to you again. He said you'd be getting some kind of apology too. That Leslie Potts must be some important man to have a lawyer like that. It must have cost a fortune to have him come all the way to

Della's house. And in the evening, too.'

Lee was trying to take all this in.

'Are you sure about all this, Kyle?'

'Sure as sure. I was there, man!'

'You see, Lee,' smiled Ruby. 'I told you they could-n't touch you.'

'So they won't come back?'

'If they come back, man, they'll be up to their necks in doodoo with that lawyer around.'

There was a moment's silence.

'Lee, if you don't get dry soon, you won't live long enough to enjoy being free of police harassment,' said Ruby firmly, and with a whoop all three of them began to race to Della's.

It was Mum who answered the door. For a moment she stared at them open-mouthed. Then she did something Lee hadn't seen her do for years. She began to laugh. She put her hands on her hips and leaned back laughing. She clutched her belly and laughed and laughed.

At school, in the form room, Lee discovered that rumours of his rescuing his dad had spread through the class. He was subjected to a barrage of questions, comments, screams and backslaps. He was relieved when the form teacher came in and he was able to slip quietly into his seat beside Vivienne.

'You're almost one of the gang today,' she said.

'Not really,' said Lee. 'Anyway, tomorrow it'll be back to normal.'

'Will that be a good or bad thing?'

Lee thought for a minute.

'Good, probably.'

Then suddenly, and without knowing he was going to do it, he added, 'Would you like to go to the cinema on Saturday?'

Vivienne stared at him in surprise.

Oh no, he thought, how stupid. Why did I say that?

'On one condition,' she said, looking very serious.

'What?' Lee was intrigued, hopeful.

'We don't go to see *Superman*,' she replied, laughing.

Kate Saksena

Kate Saksena was born in Bristol and educated at Warwick and Exeter Universities. Kate has spent most of her career teaching in south London and is now an Education Adviser. She lives in Bromley with her two teenage children.

Hite is Kate Saksena's second novel – her first, *Love, Shelley*, was published in 2003.

By the same author

Love
Shelley
KATE

To order from Bookpost PO Box 29 Douglas Isle of Man IM99 1BQ www.bookpost.co.uk
email: bookshop@enterprise.net fax: 01624 837033 tel: 01624 836000

BLOOMSBURY

www.bloomsbury.com